The Ghost Files

Volume 2

By Apryl Baker

The Ghost Files - V2

Limitless Publishing, LLC
Kailua, HI 96734
www.limitlesspublishing.com

Formatting: Limitless Publishing

ISBN-13: 978-1-68058-060-0
ISBN-10: 1-68058-060-4

Dedication

This one is for all my Watty Fans. You guys made this series and I appreciate you all so much.

Chapter One

"Go away," I hiss, trying to ignore the elderly lady staring at me. Her eyes are so clouded with cataracts it's hard to determine their color. Iron gray hair hangs in stringy waves down her back. The ratty old nightgown she's wearing has stains on it. Her lips thin at my whispered command.

"Mattie Hathaway, did you turn the air conditioner down again?"

I wince at the anger in Joan's voice. She's determined to keep the power bill at or below fifty bucks a month, which means we suffocate in the Charlotte heat. The ghost opens her mouth again, and I glare her into silence. Every freaking time one of them shows up and the temperature takes a nosedive, I get blamed for turning down the thermostat. Ghosts are good for nothing except causing me trouble.

It's not like I can come out and tell her it's not my fault, it's the ghost. She'd ship me off to the loony bin so fast my head would spin. I don't go around confessing I've been able to see the little

1

buggers since my mom tried to kill me when I was five.

"Why the hell is it so cold in here?" Joan demands, coming into what she calls the living room, but is more like a corner of a box.

The tiny, cramped apartment looks clean on the surface. The walls hold no decorations, and the furniture is plain and utilitarian. The gray carpet has a few spots, but otherwise is clean, but that's only because I clean it. Busted up hands or not, she makes me work.

Joan Myers, my latest foster mother, does not impress me. She's in her mid-forties, twenty pounds overweight, and her bottle blonde hair is messy. Her face has a permanent frown on it. As bad as she looks, Joan can't be worse than the foster mother who turned out to be a serial killer and tried to kill me.

Joan's voice is high and nasally like she's on the powder train. I so hope she's not a hidden junkie. I won't deal with that ever again. My mom was a heroin addict, and I know what that does to a person. I refuse to put up with it. Although most junkies are paper thin, Joan here isn't afraid to overindulge, so maybe I'm wrong. I haven't actually found any drugs…yet. I've only been here for two weeks.

"Don't know." I shrug and flip the page in *Star Magazine*. Seems Kim Kardashian is trying to use her kid for even more press coverage. North? Really? Why would she name the poor kid that? I shake my head in disgust. Celebrities.

Joan stalks over to the thermostat and lets out a

string of curse words. I'm pretty sure the thermostat is still set on eighty. She starts mumbling about broken things and hauls up the phone to call the building's super. I feel sorry for the poor man. Joan can be a pain in the rear when she wants to be.

My ghost seems to take offense to me ignoring her and gets right up in my face. I cringe. I hate it when they touch me. The cold they bring with them hurts, but more than that, I can feel what they're feeling. This old lady is desperate for her son to know she forgives him for what he did to her. Judging by the cigarette burn scars on her arms, I'm not so sure she should forgive him.

"Not now," I whisper and glance at Joan, who is still arguing with the super.

"Please," she wails. *"He needs to know that I forgive him."*

Since I started talking to the spooks a few months ago, they all seem to think I'm their personal messenger. Uh, no. I tried ignoring them again, like I used to, but it's useless. They know I can see them now. Ghosts are the worst gossips I've ever seen.

"If you freaking don't leave me alone right now, I *will* contact your son and tell him you despise him and will *never* forgive him," I tell her. Not that I will, mind you, but sometimes being mean is the only way to get them to leave me alone. I am not freaking Jennifer Love Hewitt from that stupid show. This is my life, and I refuse to be Ghost Girl.

She stares at me in horror and then pops out. There one minute, gone the next. The room starts to warm up the instant she's gone. Joan stops talking, aware of the change in temperature. I pretend to be engrossed in my magazine, but peek at her. She's frowning at me. I'm pretty sure she knows something is going on, and it's my fault, but she's just not sure what it is.

My stomach growls, but it's not time for dinner. Joan told me my first day here I was allowed breakfast and dinner. Anything else was off limits. Food's expensive, she'd said. Evil, selfish woman. How much can it cost for a pack of bologna and a loaf of bread? It's not like she's starving herself, either. She stuffs her face all day.

I abandon my magazine and head into the hole that serves as my room. Better there than here staring longingly at the fridge. My room is tiny— barely a closet, and empty. There's a bed, a nightstand, and a dresser. That's it. My discarded sketchpad and pencils decorate the top of the dresser. I haven't been able to draw since Mrs. Olson destroyed my hands.

My hands shake slightly as I try to stop myself from thinking of Mrs. Olson. She'd been my foster mother, one of the ones I'd truly liked. She made us all think she cared about us, and in her own sick way, maybe she did. Problem was she had split personalities, and one of them was a serial killer. She'd killed my foster sister, Sally, and when I was close to discovering the truth, she'd taken me, held me captive, and tortured me.

Sighing, I open my laptop, the one thing Joan couldn't take from me. I secretly charged the battery up at night under my bed. Thankfully, there's an outlet behind the headboard. She warned me not to waste electricity on something I could very well go to the library and use. Selfish cow. Not that I have internet; she won't pay for it.

Yes! Three unsecured networks are available. I love people who don't know that they need to set up secure networks. I giggle like a blonde flirting with a jock. Rolling my eyes at the image, I piggyback one of the connections so I can at least check my email.

There's one from my best friend, Meg. She's got some week-long super-secret event planned for my birthday. Joan was not being very cooperative about it, so Meg being Meg, had her dad, the mayor, call Joan. Not that I'm looking forward to it, exactly, but at this point, I'm going stir crazy. School is out for the summer, and I have nowhere to go except the library, and I stay as far away from there as I can. Too many ghosts. It makes my head hurt when they all bombard me.

I frown as I read her email. She's being very cryptic, which makes me nervous. What is she up to, and why do I need to pack boots? She knows I don't do outdoors. If she thinks she's dragging me hiking or camping…

"Mattie!"

What does the old hag want now?

I close my laptop and trudge back into the living room, where I stop dead for all of two-point-five seconds, then I launch myself at the guy studying Joan with calculating eyes. I can't believe it. It's Officer Dan.

He catches me easily and laughs at me. His brown eyes are full of warmth. They always thaw out some of the ice that lives inside me. I have never understood the weird relationship Dan Richards and I share, but I value it more than anything else in the world. He'd believed me about Sally when no one else would, and helped me to solve her murder. Not only that, but he'd saved my life when Mrs. Olson had captured me.

"Happy birthday, Squirt." He grins at my scrunched-up face at the nickname he'd given me. He knows I hate it, but then he's not fond of his nickname, either.

"It's not my birthday until tomorrow, Officer Dan," I tell him sassily, but refuse to let him go. I missed him so much. He's been away at Quantico training with the FBI. After all the work he did to bring down a serial killer—Mrs. Olson—he's gotten a lot of attention at the Charlotte PD. He's not supposed to be back for another two weeks, though. "What are you doing here?"

"Nancy called me."

Uh oh. If Nancy called him, it's serious. She's been very quiet recently, urging me to be on my best behavior, but I haven't felt like being anything but me.

"Mattie, are you going to introduce your…friend?"

I cringed at Joan's tone of voice. Leave it to her to jump to all the wrong conclusions. "Joan, this is Officer Dan Richards from the Charlotte Police Department. Dan, this is my latest foster mother, Joan Myers."

We both notice the alarm that crosses Joan's face. Well, fudgepops, maybe she is on the crack train. I so don't need that. Dan frowns at her, and she quickly excuses herself.

"Okay, Mattie, what's going on?" he asks, his eyes troubled.

"Nothing's going on," I deny. What did Nancy tell him?

"Uh-huh. Care to tell me why you screamed at a five-year-old?"

I close my eyes briefly and sit on the stained couch. I can't believe she told him about that. Mark had asked me to color with him, and I'd gotten frustrated when he'd laughed because I couldn't stay inside the lines. My anger had bubbled over, and I'd taken it out on him. Not my finest moment. I'd apologized to the kid, but apparently our foster parents refused to have a "violent" child in the home. It actually wasn't a bad place. They seemed to be nice folks. That one was all on me. Since getting out of the hospital, I've taken my anger out on a lot people who didn't deserve it. I know that, but I can't seem to help it.

In all honesty, the last three homes I'd been placed in had been really, *really* good ones, but I can't seem to stem the bitterness spewing out of my mouth these days. I'd wrecked my own chances at a good foster home not once, not twice, but three times in the last two months.

Dan sits down and takes my hands. They surround my smaller ones, and I marvel at how tiny they look compared to his. He turns them over and examines the scars left over from the string of surgeries I'd had to undergo to correct the damage Mrs. Olson had inflicted. She'd smashed them both

7

with a sledgehammer while I was tied down, unable to move. Thinking about it gives me the willies. I'd taken the bandages off earlier and forgot to put them back on. The bandages help to relieve the pain, and they help me to forget sometimes how I got the scars.

No. I am stronger than she is. She will not beat me. It's a mantra I whisper over and over every time I wake up screaming. Don't get me wrong, I'm a tough cookie—had to be, growing up in the foster care system—but being tortured is something even I can't shake off. It haunts me.

Dan, however, brings out my vulnerable side. I hate him for it some days, bless him for it others. He makes me feel safe enough to be vulnerable.

"Well?" he prompts when I don't answer.

"Look, it's not a big deal. I apologized to the kid."

"Yeah, Mattie, it kinda *is* a big deal," he refutes softly. "Nancy said if you get kicked out of one more home, the only place she has left to put you is a group home."

"What?" A group home? My gut twists at the thought. The only group home I'd ever been in was Hartford House. They'd closed it down shortly after I arrived. It was also the place Mrs. Olson had staged her torture room. Group homes have an entirely different meaning for me now. I can't go to a group home. I won't. I'll run away before that happens.

"Squirt, I know you're angry about everything…"

"Angry?" I laugh harshly and hold my damaged

hands up to him. "I can't even hold a crayon and color inside the lines, Dan. Angry is not the right word."

He sighs and I glare at him, daring him to say anything. He knows what I've gone through. Dan is the only person I've told everything.

"Look, Squirt. There's not a lot that Nancy can do if you get kicked out of here. Will you promise me to try to behave and curb your temper?"

I know he's worried. I see it in his eyes and can sense the frustration in him when he runs his fingers through his short cropped brown hair. He'd even tried to get his parents to take me in as a foster kid, but his mom didn't want to deal with an "emotionally scarred, potentially violent girl." I don't think his mom has ever been fond of me, but I don't really know why. I'm always on my best behavior around her, and I'm polite, but she's never really friendly. His dad is a different story. He adores me, smart mouth and all. I think if it had been up to him, I'd be sitting in the Richards' living room right now instead of this cesspool.

"I promise to try not to be too lippy," I agree reluctantly.

He rolls his eyes, and I laugh. "I think it's the best I'm going to get from you, isn't it?"

"Sure is." I grin. "So, you came all the way from Quantico to talk to me about my bad behavior?"

"And to give you your birthday present."

Present? I perk up.

Standing, he goes over to the door and picks up a box on the table I hadn't noticed earlier. It's small, but it's wrapped in garish pink and silver with little happy birthday logos all over it. I raise my eyebrows. Dan knows I'm not a pink girl.

He shrugs and hands it over. The crooked paper is a sure sign he wrapped it himself. I smile. I figured he'd have had the salesgirl do it for him. Not to be one to sit and admire his lopsided wrapping, I tear it open and nearly squeal like a girl. It's a phone, and not just any phone, but the one I wanted. The Samsung Galaxy S4. Oh. My. God. He did not!

Then my momentary euphoria dies. I can't afford the service on it. The hag keeps all the money for herself and won't let me have a phone. Why spend money on a cell phone when I can use the perfectly good phone in the living room? Evil bat.

"Dan, thank you so much, but…"

"No buts, Squirt. You need a phone, with as much trouble as you get yourself into. When you told me one of your foster dads 'accidentally' lost yours, I figured I'd get you a good one."

"You don't understand," I say, frustrated. "I can't afford the service."

He gives me the patented Officer Dan grin. "It's covered. Don't worry about it, Squirt."

"Uh, no, it's not," I tell him. "You can barely afford your rent, let alone two cell phone bills."

"I got a raise, Mattie. Don't argue about your birthday gift. It's not nice."

"I'm not a nice person, or did you forget that, *Officer Dan*?" I ask.

He shakes his head, and his brown eyes darken with anger. "Mattie, the last time you didn't have a phone, you got kidnapped and tortured."

The old boy has a point there.

"And since you won't promise me not to go running off after a ghost again—with no backup—you're keeping the phone!"

We glare at each other, neither willing to lose the staring contest. He's such a dork sometimes.

"I hate owing people, Dan," I finally say. "You know that."

"It has a built-in wifi connection," he wheedles. "You can have internet for the laptop anywhere you go with wifi."

"And I do have backup," I tell him. I have Eric. Eric, or Mirror Boy, as I call him sometimes, had been the first of Mrs. Olson's victims, and he'd done everything he could to keep me from danger, down to accidentally hurting me. He stuck around to keep me out of trouble, or so he says. I think he just likes to peek at me in the shower, even if he denies it.

"A ghost does not constitute backup, Mattie," he argues, "especially if no one can see or hear him but you."

"Are you really gonna sit here and argue with me on my birthday?"

"It's not your birthday yet."

It's my turn to sigh. "I'll keep the danged phone, already!"

"Good," he snaps.

"Fine," I growl.

"I swear, you're worse than two-year-olds arguing over a toy." Mr. Richards laughs when he walks in. I hadn't noticed Dan left the front door open. We'd been arguing so loudly, neither of us heard him come in. Mr. Richards doesn't look a thing like Dan, but then neither does his mother. They'd adopted him when he was a baby. Mr. Richards is tall, stately, and his blue eyes twinkle with laughter.

We both turn baleful eyes on him. We are *not* children, despite the fact we're arguing like them. He laughs out loud at our murderous expressions.

"Go get your things, Mattie," he says with a chuckle. "We're going out to dinner to celebrate your birthday."

My stomach growls noisily at the very mention of food, and they both give me frowns of concern. I jump up and head for my room. I'm not turning down free food.

I open the door to my room and run straight for my purse, lying on the bed. Before I can turn around, the room starts to freeze up. I don't have time for this. I'm hungry, dang it. I turn around to yell at the ghost and stop, the words dying on my lips.

It stares at me from the barren corner across the room. The entire area around it is shrouded in black, making the pale face staring at me even more stark. Long, straggly black hair flows around, shoulders hunched in, like its preparing to attack. I take an involuntary step back at the rage and hate emanating from it.

When it looks at me, I want to run. Its eyes are pools of liquid darkness, a black so deep it scares me. The thing's mouth opens, and black liquid begins to trickle out, running steadily to pool at its feet before starting to slowly leach toward me. I

12

jump on the bed, my eyes never leaving the thing standing across from me.

Its head jerks in a motion that reminds me of those crazy people you see on TV who are insane and constantly twitch. The fingers are curled like claws, and they clench repeatedly. It simply stares at me. I want to scream at it, to demand it leave me alone, but my voice fails me. There are very few things in this world that can scare me, and standing across from me is the thing that just made the top of the list.

With a twisted jerk of its entire body, it starts to shuffle forward. I inch back, intending to jump off the bed, but before I can so much as move, it's standing in front of me, the stench coming from it making me gag.

It touches me.

Chapter Two

I can't breathe.

I can't move.

I can't see past the darkness of the eyes staring into mine.

My lungs burn, and I want to cough, but I can't. All I can do is kneel on the bed and scream, but no sound escapes my lips. Liquid, hot and foul, fills my mouth. It seeps out, running down my chin. The stench is unbearable, but I'm frozen, unable to defend against the hatred emanating from the thing in front of me. I can feel its need to hurt me, to consume me.

"Squirt…what the…what…is…*that*?"

Dan sees it?

"Mattie!"

I focus on the panic in his voice. This *thing* might hurt him. I won't let it hurt him. I manage to close my eyes, and I can breathe. It can't control me if I'm not looking at it. A wail unlike anything I've ever heard bombards me. I can hear Dan shouting something, but if I open my eyes, I'll be defenseless, and I will not be defenseless. Not ever again.

Rotten eggs. Ghosts don't smell like rotten eggs. What is this thing?

Cold lips press against mine, and I open my eyes, startled, repulsed. Those liquid pools of ink try to pull me back in, but I can see Dan. He looks scared, and that look grounds me in a way nothing else could have.

"Go away," I tell it, my voice not as strong as I want, but at least I manage to get the words out.

It hisses.

"I said go away!" I shout, my voice strong and loud in the quiet of my room.

Another hiss, and it backs away. I start to relax, but then it turns, and it's standing next to Dan. He stumbles back, and in his haste to get away, falls flat on his butt. His eyes widen as it bends toward him. The brown in them have gone black in panic.

"No!" I jump down and grab the only thing I can get my hands on, my laptop, and swing at it. It passes right through the thing and slams into the doorframe.

"Dan? Mattie?" Mr. Richards calls. "What is going on in there?"

With a hiss, the thing flickers and fades. It's not like a ghost. Ghosts pop in and out, but this thing, it was like watching an image fade in and out of a snowy channel on TV. It jerked and jumped before bleeding into the air around it.

"Daniel Aaron Richards, what are you doing?"

We both swivel our heads to see Mr. Richards glaring at his son. I know what this looks like. Dan is on his butt, and I'm standing over him with a busted laptop. Oh, God, my laptop... *NoNoNoNoNo*!

"D-Dad..."

"My fault, Mr. Richards," I tell him, my voice still shaky. "I saw a cockroach the size of a small mouse crawling up the doorframe. I slapped it with the laptop and Dan dived out of the way."

"Cockroach?" He frowns and glances over the room.

Dan nods. "Yeah, Dad. What she said."

Mr. Richards frowns at both of us, not believing a word of it, but there's not a lot he can do. He hauls his son up and gives him a good hard stare, which causes Dan to look at the floor. He's such a bad liar. I get the same look, but I stare back at Dan's dad with complete innocence. He shakes his head and mutters something about peas and pods.

"If you two are done goofing off, I'd like to get going," he says and starts to walk down the hall. "We have reservations."

"What the hell was that?" Dan whispers as soon as his dad is out of earshot.

"No clue," I tell him. "You *did* see it though, right?"

He nods.

Wow. Officer Dan, the most emphatic non-believer I've ever met, saw a ghost. Well, not a ghost, but it was something, and he *did* see it.

"We'll call Dr. Olivet as soon as we can ditch Dad," he says. "Come on, let's get out of here."

He doesn't have to tell me twice. No way do I want to spend alone time in my room any time

16

The Ghost Files — V2

soon.

Dan's rickety old beat-up Ford truck is parked in front of the building with his Dad's brand-new Lexus behind it. Dan and I head for the truck, but his dad cuts us off by asking us to ride with him. We share a shuttered look, which causes Mr. Richards's frown to deepen. My eyes widen when I realize what he's thinking. Uh, no.

"That's fine, Mr. Richards," I tell him. "Your car is way more comfy than Officer Dan's mutant truck."

"It is not a mutant!" Dan's outraged look distracts his dad into laughing.

"How many different shades of color are on it?" I challenge. I can see primer, red, and brown with only a quick glance. I know he said he was doing some bodywork on it, but right now it just looks like a mess.

"Don't tease him, Mattie." Mr. Richards hides a smile. "He's overly sensitive about Myrtle."

"Myrtle?" I almost choke on my laughter.

"That was her name when I bought her," he defends, his face red.

"Come on, kids, get in the car."

Dan and I pile in the back seat, which earns us another speculative look from his dad. This time, Dan picks up on it and shakes his head.

The car moves into traffic, and I sit back to enjoy the ride. His dad's Lexus is a nice car and it's not often I get to ride in something so luxurious.

"There's something I wanted to talk to you about before we get to the restaurant, Mattie."

My attention is drawn back to Mr. Richards. He

17

sounds very serious.

"I've been thinking about your situation for a while now," he says. "Given that you're turning seventeen tomorrow, have you thought about emancipation?"

My eyes widen. I have thought it, constantly, but it's not something I can do, not given my situation.

"Yes, sir, I have, but I still have two more surgeries on my hands and a ton of physical therapy. I can't pay for that."

"Well, if the Department of Health and Human Services agreed to cover your medical expenses as related to injuries sustained while in their care, would you do it?"

Sometimes I forget Dan's father is a lawyer, and then he goes and reminds me with the professional tone he usually reserves for Dan.

"Dad, she wouldn't have anywhere to go, to stay. She doesn't have any money..." Dan trails off, his eyes widening, and then a grin splits his face.

"And that is exactly why I was hesitant to broach the topic with her." Mr. Richards sighs. "It wouldn't be at all proper, Daniel."

"What?" I ask, confused at the almost silent conversation going on between them with facial expressions.

"Dad knows I'll let you sleep on my couch."

"She's only sixteen..."

"Seventeen tomorrow," Dan reminds his father.

"Whether it's the legal age of consent or not doesn't mean I'm going to condone it—"

"Whoa, Dad, hold up there," Dan interrupts. "You got the wrong idea. Mattie and I are not…we're friends…we…"

"I'm not blind, son."

My eyes keep darting back and forth between the two of them, fascinated. It always amazes me to watch them interact. It reminds me of what I missed out on growing up.

"Yeah, you kinda are, Dad." Dan shakes his head. "She's…she means a lot to me, but—"

"But nothing…" Mr. Richards sighs. "You two are not going down that road, at least not until she's in college."

"Do I get a say in this?" I ask.

"No." They both give me glares.

"Why even bring it up, then, Dad?" Dan asks, frustrated. "You know she can't afford to be on her own. She can't work, not with her hands still damaged. They have bandages on them more often than not. She has to have a way to get to all her physical therapy appointments, school, *and* she has to be able to feed herself, which she can't do without working!"

"Until today, I *had* thought about her staying with you," Mr. Richards says. "You two act more like brother and sister, but then sometimes, I don't know, I see more there than that."

"Mr. Richards," I say, my voice soft. "Dan and I are not involved, if that's what you're thinking. He would never take advantage of me like that. You raised a good man."

"But you could be, Mattie, if in close proximity for a long time," Mr. Richards replies. "The look you two were sharing a little while ago, you were hiding something from me."

"Yeah, we were hiding something," I tell him, "but not that."

"What were you hiding, Mattie?"

I say the first thing that comes to mind. "I think Joan is on the powder train."

"She's on drugs?" His dad swerves the car at that statement, and I think for two seconds we are gonna end up splattered against the semi-truck in the other lane, but he recovers almost instantly.

"I don't know." I shake my head. "I haven't found any drugs, but I've been around enough junkies to recognize the signs."

"Plus, I don't think she's getting fed enough," Dan tells his dad, and my stomach picks that moment to rumble.

"How would you know that, Dan?" I ask. I haven't seen him in over a month.

"You've lost weight, Squirt," he says.

"Could be stress," I deny. I can't get removed from this foster home, and he knows it.

He snorts when my stomach growls again.

Mr. Richards's face is troubled, but we are pulling into the parking lot of Jake's, my favorite little hole-in-the-wall in Charlotte. They serve the absolute best burgers in town. And their chili fries…ohmygod! So good!

"We'll talk about this on the way home, kids," Mr. Richards pulls into a parking spot. We both wince at the word "kids." We are not kids.

The restaurant is packed when we enter, but that doesn't stop me from seeing Meg, my best friend, jumping up and down, and hearing everyone shouting, "Happy Birthday!" I smile. I've never,

ever had a birthday party. I glance up at Dan, who is grinning like an idiot.

"Happy birthday, Squirt," he whispers in my ear.

"Thank you, Officer Dan." It's the nicest thing anyone has ever done for me.

Someone grabs my hand, and I'm pulled away from Dan. I look up to see him rolling his eyes at Mason as he drags me toward the table. I'd met Mason a few months ago, and he has been a good friend since.

Mason stops a few feet from the table and turns to look at me. I blink and blink again. He looks kinda blurry and distorted.

It hurts my eyes for a minute, but then I can see…Eric?

Chapter Three

Ohmygosh! Eric...how? He grins at the question on my face, and instead of heading for the table, he leads me toward the back where the restrooms are. I see Meg wink at me knowingly...she has no idea.

As soon as we're out of earshot, Eric wraps me in a hug and whispers, "Happy early birthday, Mattie!"

I stare up into Eric's blue eyes, and I feel the butterflies start in my stomach—no, scratch that. They're on a marathon flutter-a-thon. Why is it that the only person who can make me feel like this is dead? So not fair.

"How?" I ask.

He smiles that cocky smile I've grown so fond of. I'd met him while still at Mrs. Olson's when he'd tried to scare me away from finding out what happened to my foster sister. In his eagerness to keep me safe, he'd accidentally landed me in the hospital. Back then, I'd nicknamed him Mirror Boy, as that was the first place I'd seen him—in the mirror with his face so mangled, it was hard to tell he was a guy. Now, I only see him as the cute boy he'd been before Mrs. Olson killed him.

"I hijacked a body."

I roll my eyes. "Obviously, but how?"

"It's not as easy as you think," he tells me. "I actually tried to body jump Dan over there, but that didn't work out so well. He's got some kind of internal shielding that makes me bounce right off. Freaky weird. Mason here was easy. He has an open mind, and it let me in without any resistance."

"You didn't hurt Mason, did you?" Mason is a really, really nice guy and I don't want him to suffer, no matter how excited I am to see Eric in the flesh.

"Nah, he won't even remember this," Eric shakes his head and his face turns serious. "You have to promise me something, Mattie."

"What?" I ask.

"That you won't get into any kind of ghost trouble for at least a week."

"A week? Why a week?"

"It takes a lot of energy to possess someone," he says. "It's gonna take me at least that long to recover once I leave this guy's body. He has the hots for you, by the way, and I don't mean only a crush. He has it *bad*."

"Why would you do this if it costs you so much?" I demand.

"Glad you asked that, Mathilda Hathaway." He smiles, and there is no trace of Mason in his face. I only see Eric. He leans in before I can do anything and kisses me.

For all of five seconds, I freeze. I mean…wow.

Then emotions flood me, and I realize I'm feeling Eric's emotions. Even though he's in a body, he *is* still a ghost, and I can feel that part of him. He's elated, triumphant, and…and happy. This is all he's wanted to do since he first saw me. I see all this in a flash, and it overshadows everything I feel.

Now, does that mean I don't enjoy it? Heck no. The boy can kiss, and kiss well.

"Mason!"

Eric ignores Dan's shout. So do I, for that matter, which only makes Dan mad. He yanks us apart and glares holes into Eric. "What do you think you're doing?"

"Giving Mattie a birthday kiss," he replies with his cocky smile. "What's it to you?"

"What did I tell you about this? She needs time to get over everything."

"Chill, man." Eric winks at me. "Mason won't remember this in the morning."

Dan frowns, and I laugh. "Um, Officer Dan, that's not Mason. That's Eric. He kinda hijacked Mason's body for my party."

Dan's facial expressions range from outright disbelief to a kind of comical horror. He was forced to admit I can see ghosts, but a part of him still doesn't want to believe it. Though after that thing we saw in my bedroom…

"Come on!" Dan whisper-shouts. "You can't really expect me to believe that…that…that…"

"Dan, didn't you agree that when it came to ghosts, you'd trust me?" I ask.

He nods reluctantly.

"Then when I tell you that this is Eric, this really

is Eric."

Dan opens his mouth as if to argue then thinks better of it. Smart boy. After that thing from earlier, you'd think he'd be a little more believing…wait, maybe…

"Eric, what kind of ghost smells like rotten eggs?" I ask. His kisses had momentarily distracted me.

"None." He frowns. "Where did you smell that?"

"There was this thing in my bedroom," I tell him. "At first, I thought it was a random ghost, but it wasn't like my normal ones. It touched me, and I couldn't breathe, couldn't move, couldn't do anything. If it wasn't for Dan, I don't know what might have happened." I shudder at the thought. "It was weird. Its face was all distorted, almost a solid white, but its eyes were black."

"Don't forget that nasty black goo that oozed out of its mouth." Dan grimaces.

"Goo?" Eric asks. "Did you see it, Dan?"

He nods.

"Mattie, that's not a ghost. I'm not sure what it is, especially if your boy here can see it, but you need to stay away from it."

"Not like I have a choice, Eric," I tell him. "And Dan is not my boy."

"If you say so." He laughs. "We'd better get back to the table. They look like they're going to hunt us down if we don't."

True enough. Meg looks like she wants to burst over here and demand answers. She has a thing for Dan, but refuses to act on it because she thinks I might like him. Makes her a great friend in my book. Truth is, I *might* have a thing for him, I just don't know myself. Mr. Richards could be right in that having us live together could force the issue. The real question is, do I want to find out?

"Are we late?" I hear a breathless voice and turn to see Mary Cross and her mother coming over to our table. Mary was the only one of Mrs. Olson's victims I actually managed to save. She and I shared a hospital room for over a month while we recovered from our torture. To say we were friends would be a gross understatement. You don't survive something like that and just be friends. Mary's family, same as Dan, at least to me.

"No, you're not late." I grin and give her a hug, careful of her left arm. It was shattered in so many places they're still doing reconstructive surgery on it.

"Come on, guys, sit down." Meg waves at the waiter to take orders.

Megan is the first best friend I've ever had. I've always made sure I was in with the popular crowd at school, no matter what district my new foster home was in, but I'd never actually been "friends" with any of them. Meg refused to let me get away with that. She bowled me over and forced me to be her friend. That's just the kind of person she is, though. Everyone's sweetheart. Not at all like me, the messed up foster kid who grew up learning to survive by herself. I'm still not sure why Meg and I are friends, we simply are.

"So, did you get boots?" she asks, laughter twinkling in her green eyes.

"I swear to all that is holy, if you think you're

taking me hiking *or* camping…"

She bursts out laughing. "Do I *look* like an outdoorsy person to you?"

Well, no. Meg is definitely not an outdoorsy person. She's a mall kind of girl. "Then why do I need boots?"

"It was on the list of needed things." She shrugs. "Anyway, I can't wait! We fly out tomorrow morning."

"Fly?" I feel a bit of panic at the word. Like in an airplane? My eyes go wide at the thought of twisting, burning metal, screaming people…uh, no. "I don't fly, Meg."

"Oh, my God!" Meg exclaims. "Don't tell me the great and fearless Mattie Hathaway is afraid of flying."

"I'm not afraid." I am, but no way will I admit that. "I simply prefer to keep my feet on the ground, is all."

Dan snorts, not believing a word of it.

The waitress saves me from having to answer. She drops by to take drink orders and hands out menus. Mine is easy, double bacon cheeseburger and chili cheese fries. My mouth waters just thinking about it.

I look up to see my social worker, Nancy Moriarity, coming to our table. She's wearing a smile the size of a kid who just stole the last chocolate chip cookie and waving a manila envelope, which sets Mary squealing. What in the world? I look from one to the other.

Eric leans in and whispers, "I think you're about to get the best birthday gift ever."

"Why? What do you know?" I ask suspiciously.

He only grins at me, which causes me to stick my tongue out at him, and he bursts out laughing.

"Happy birthday, Mattie!" Nancy beams at me, and the waiter brings her a chair. Once she's seated, she hands the manila envelope over to Mary's mother. "Do you want to tell her, or should I?"

"You're coming to live with us!" Mary nearly bounces out of her seat before the words are even out of Nancy's mouth.

My head snaps around to her. "What?"

She is grinning like the Cheshire Cat. "We're taking you home with us, Mattie."

I frown at her then look at Nancy.

"We didn't say anything to you before because we didn't want to get your hopes up," she tells me. "Mrs. Cross applied to be a foster parent so she and Mary could give you a proper home."

A home? A real home? For me?

Mrs. Cross smiles at me from across the table. "You gave me back my daughter, Mattie. The least I can do is to give you a home where you can be yourself and not worry about…temperature spikes."

My eyes go a little round at that.

Mary nods. "I remember everything, Mattie. Mom understands."

Dan reaches over and squeezes my hand. I know he can see the panic on my face, and he understands how hard this is for me. I've never had a home before, never even contemplated it. Now, here I am, being offered one by people who understand that I can see ghosts and won't call me a freak.

I feel the onset of tears and force them back. I do

not cry. I *will not* cry. Please don't let me cry.

"That is, if you want to come live with us?" Mrs. Cross asks me softly, seeing the same panic Dan saw.

"Of course, she does, Mom," Mary tells her then glances at me. "Don't you?"

"I…" What do I say?

Nancy is staring at me with growing concern.

"I think she needs some air," Dan says and then hauls me up. "We'll be right back." Before I can blink, he's dragging me through the restaurant and outside, where I get wrapped in the biggest bear hug imaginable.

"Just breathe, Squirt."

"What do I do?" I ask, my face buried in his shirt.

"What do you want to do?"

"I've never had a home before," I whisper. "What if I mess it up? What if I can't…"

"Mattie, you won't mess it up."

"I always mess things up." I shake my head. "I screwed up the last couple foster homes I was in, and they were all really, really nice ones. I can't help myself, Dan. I think I'm too broken."

"Mattie?"

I lift my face out of Dan's shirt and see Mrs. Cross standing about a foot away from us. Her blue eyes are warm and full of compassion. She looks exactly like Mary.

"I'm sorry if we shocked you."

"I…"

"I heard you telling Dan you were afraid you'd mess things up," she says with a smile. "If you are at all like Mary, you're still angry and bitter over what happened to you, and I understand that. I can deal with it. You brought my daughter home, alive. That is a gift that I can never repay you for. Will you at least let me give you a home where you'll be safe and cared for and loved? Where you won't have to hide what you can do?"

"You believe I can see...?"

She nods, her face solemn. "Mary told me everything, and if even half of what she said is true, then you're a very special person, Mattie. You saved my daughter. Please let me save you."

"You really want me to live with you?" I ask softly.

"Mary has spent the last month getting your room ready." She laughs. "We can go pick out anything you don't agree with. My daughter loves purple and assumes everyone else does as well."

I can't stop the grimace...purple...shudder.

Dan's chest rumbles with laughter. He'd brought me a purple teddy bear in the hospital, and I'd promptly had Meg throw it at him since my hands had been bandaged up. He knows about my aversion to anything pink or purple.

"So, what do you say, honey?" Mrs. Cross asks. "Do you think you'd like to try living with me and Mary for a little while?"

I nod. "I'd like that very much."

"Come back in when you're ready," she tells me then goes inside the restaurant.

"You okay, Squirt?" Dan asks.

"I think maybe I will be." I smile up into his warm, puppy dog eyes. "It's a home, Dan, a real home."

His forehead presses against mine, and all I can see are his eyes. "You deserve a home, Mattie."

Neither of us smile or move in that moment. I can see a question in his eyes, and I know he can see the same one in mine. Is this a step we want to take?

Maattiieee...

Shivers run up my spine, and my stomach knots up. The voice is full of ice, and it surrounds me. Even Dan stiffens up a bit, but I don't know if it's in reaction to my face or if he senses something too.

I peek around him, looking for the source of the voice.

"What's wrong?" he asks, turning to look himself.

The thing from my bedroom is calling me, knows my name. It's standing across the street in front of the entrance to an apartment complex that takes up most of the city block. It's an old building, probably as old as the city itself. It jerks, and it's standing in the street.

Another jerk, and it's only a few feet away from us.

Maattiieee...

It reaches for me.

Chapter Four

I waste no time running. I have no clue what the thing is, nor does Eric know. With Dan in tow, I dash back inside and sneak a peek out the restaurant windows. It's still standing in the street, but it's not coming any closer. Doesn't mean I'm safe, only means I have a minute until it figures out what it wants to do.

"Mattie?" Dan is frowning at me.

"The thing from before, in my bedroom," I whisper, still staring out the window. "Do you see it?"

Dan glances out the window. At first, I don't think he sees anything, but the longer he looks, the more perplexed his face becomes. Then it goes to downright horror.

"We're calling Olivet as soon as we can," he says quietly. "Why can I see it?"

"How should I know?"

"You're the ghost girl. You're supposed to know these things."

I stare at him as if he's lost his mind. "Since

when do I know everything because I can see the freaking things?"

"Mattie, Dan, what's going on?" Eric asks, and we both whirl to see him standing there with a question on his face.

"Do you see that thing?" I point out the window at the black form in the street.

Eric walks closer and looks out the window. After a minute, he turns and shakes his head. "I don't see anything, Mattie."

"It's standing right there!" Dan almost shouts, but catches himself.

Eric shrugs. "Maybe I can't see it because Mason can't?"

"That makes no sense," I tell him. "I can see you fine, so you should be able to see that thing."

"Mattie, you can see me because you can see ghosts, and I'm a ghost who borrowed a body. While I'm in here, I'm stuck with Mason's abilities, and he *can't* see ghosts."

Dan's phone starts blaring, and he pulls it out and frowns. He walks a few feet away and starts talking.

Eric leans closer. "So, how's it going with you and Officer Dan?"

"What do you mean?"

"Mattie, I saw him almost kiss you." Eric laughs at my horrified face. "I'm not mad. In fact, I'm kinda glad. He's good for you, and you for him."

"He's too old." That, and the fact that I don't get butterflies when I think of him that way. I love Dan, I really, really do, but I don't know if it's the kind of love Eric is talking about.

"You're seventeen, Mattie. He's only three years older than you."

"But what if the only person I want is you?" I stare up into his blue eyes.

His smile is sad. "That's never going to happen, Mattie. I can't...I'm...it can't be, no matter what either of us want."

I know he's right, but that doesn't stop me from wanting it. Sad that the only person who gives me butterflies is a ghost. It's those big blue eyes of his.

"Mattie."

The serious note in Dan's voice causes me to tense up. He only uses that tone when it's something bad.

"What?" I ask, afraid of the solemn look in his eyes.

"We're skipping your birthday dinner," he says quietly. "Mas...Eric, can you let them know that Mattie and I are going to celebrate somewhere else?"

"Dan, Meg is going to pitch a fit..."

"It's about your mom, Mattie."

My mom. The woman who'd raised me and then tried to kill me when I was five. Her ghost had finally come to see me in the hospital after I'd survived Mrs. Olson's terrorfest. What she'd told me had floored me. She wasn't my mother. That's all she said before disappearing into the light. Dan had been looking into it since I told him the next day.

"Come on. That thing's not out there anymore." Dan grabs my hand. "Let's go before it comes back."

I'm feeling numb. I get bustled outside and onto a bus. Ever since my mom dropped that little bombshell on me, I've thought of little else. What did she mean? Was she an aunt, or a friend of my real mom's? Did she kidnap me? There are so many possibilities, and I've given myself migraines trying to figure out what she meant.

I know Dan has been trying to track her movements, but we'd moved all over the place when I was little. My mom never stayed in the same place more than a couple weeks. That, right there, says to me she probably kidnapped me. I'm sure Dan thinks the same thing, but he always tries to be positive about it.

"What did you find out?" I ask at last.

"Your mom moved you guys around a lot, Mattie, probably more than you even remember. It took me about four months to track her movements. You were only in Jersey about a week before she…well, before the incident."

I nod. I already know all this.

"The one place she kept going back to was New Orleans. Dad has a friend who's a PI down there. I called him, and he agreed to look into it."

"And?"

"And he wants me to come down there," he says slowly.

"Why?"

"He wouldn't say over the phone, Squirt."

"That's bad, yeah?" I ask.

"Not necessarily," he says as the bus stops a block from his apartment complex. "Come on. We'll order pizza."

"I'd rather have my burger," I grouch half-heartedly. What could be so bad that Dan would need to go to New Orleans? When we finally reach his place, I fall down on the couch, grab the fuzzy blanket he keeps especially for me, and start to tear at the frayed edges.

"Don't freak out, Squirt," he says while logging on his computer. He and I agree the only pizza worth eating is Papa John's but we both love Domino's subs.

"Dan, what if he tells you something really awful?" I ask. "What if he tells you my mom kidnapped me or...or...I don't know, something worse."

"It's going to be okay, Mattie," he says. "I promise, everything is going to be fine."

But it won't be fine. He knows it, and I know it.

"Why don't you call Dr. Olivet while I finish ordering pizza and subs, okay?"

"I don't have a phone..." I stop mid-sentence when he gives me his patented Officer Dan stare. It communicates eyes rolling and sarcastic tone, all with only a look. I grin sheepishly at him and pull my phone out of my pocket. Thankfully, I'd shoved it in my jeans pocket instead of my purse, which was still at the restaurant.

Maybe talking to the Spook Doctor about that creepy thing from earlier will distract me from thoughts of my mom and what she'd done. I'd met Dr. Olivet a few months ago when I was trying to find out what had happened to my foster sister, Sally. He was a parapsychologist who helped me understand a little bit more about my gift.

According to him, people who can see ghosts the way I can are meant to be reapers after they die. Reapers help souls get from this plane to the next by navigating through the Between, a place of shades and horrors that want to consume the energy of the newly-freed soul. That's why I can see ghosts and open a doorway to the Between. I'm a living reaper, meant to help souls cross over. Not that I want to be. I'd just as soon be normal. No one wants to be bothered with spirits popping up at unexpected times, scaring the bejeezus out of them.

In order for my gift to activate, I would have to have died at one point. Dan checked my medical records for me. When the EMTs arrived at our apartment the day my mom stabbed me eight times, I wasn't breathing. They managed to revive me, but it was long enough for my gift to come alive. I woke up to dead people everywhere.

Most people who claim to have seen a ghost will say they saw a flicker of an image or some kind of distortion in a photo. Some will even swear to have felt a ghost touch them. I can't say for certain if they did or didn't. All I know is how I see them.

To me, they are as real and substantial as the living. I see them as well as I see Dan frowning at the online ordering form across from me. Not only do I see them, I feel them too. Their feelings become my feelings, and I'm always so cold. I've never been warm since that first day I woke up in the hospital. The cold is as much a part of me now as they are.

Dr. Olivet picked up on the fifth ring. "Hello?"

"Hey, Doc, it's Mattie."

"Mattie, did you get a new number? This isn't the one I have saved in my contacts."

I nod and realize he can't see me. "Yeah, Dan bought me a new phone for my birthday."

"Your birthday is today?" he asks. "If I had known, I'd have sent you a gift."

"Don't worry about it, Doc. I need to talk to you about something Dan and I saw today."

"Of course...hold on, did you say *Dan* saw something?" The shock in his voice pretty much mirrors Dan's reaction earlier.

"Yeah, he's freaked," I tell the Doc. "I'm not sure it's a ghost." I proceed to fill him in on every encounter we've had so far with the thing. "Is it a shade, maybe?"

"No, it's not a shade, Mattie," he says quietly. Too quietly. That can't be at all good.

"Then what is it?"

"Where are you right now?" he asks instead of answering my question.

"I'm at Dan's place. Why? What is that thing, Doc?"

"Mattie, it sounds like a demon."

"A *what*?" Did he say demon? No freaking way. That thing knows my name!

That gets Dan's attention. He stops fussing with the laptop and gives me a questioning look. He so doesn't want to know.

"Calm down, Mattie," Doc says, trying to soothe me.

"Don't tell me to calm down!" I yell into the phone. "It knows my name!"

"You didn't tell me that, Mattie. It actually said

your name?"

"Why else would I be freaking out, here, Doc?" I ask sarcastically.

"Squirt, what is Dr. Olivet saying?" Dan leaves his laptop and comes to sit beside me. There is fear and concern waging a war in those gooey brown eyes of his.

"He says it's a demon," I tell him and wince at his reaction. He starts to freak out himself.

"What do you mean, a demon? And why can I see it?" He says it all in a rush, and I can barely make out the words.

"Yeah, why can Dan see it?" I ask the doc. "He can't see the ghosts, but he can see a demon?"

"Put me on speaker," Doc says. It's a new phone, and the normal speaker button isn't where it's supposed to be. Dan takes the phone from me and shows me how to do it.

"Go ahead, Doc," I say.

"First thing, you both need to calm down."

As if. What is he smoking right now if he thinks I'm calming down after he says a *demon* knows my name?

"Look, I did *not* sign up for this, Doc! Ghosts are one thing, but you're telling me demons are real? And that I've got one who has my 4-1-1? Would *you* be calm right now? I don't think so!"

"Dan, can you talk some sense into her?"

"Uh, no, don't think so, Doctor," Dan replies. "I'm right there on the freak-out train with her."

We hear him sigh. "I need to do some research, kids. Let me get back to you in a couple hours. I need to find out why Dan is seeing the demon. He shouldn't be able to. Mattie, I don't want you by yourself tonight. Do you have somewhere you can stay?"

"She can stay with me," Dan says. "We'll camp out in the living room."

"Good, good, you should probably stay together until I figure this out. I'll give you guys a call back soon."

Click.

No "goodbye" or a "hang in there." Nope, just *click*. So rude.

"We should probably at least try to stay calm," Dan says. "I mean, Dr. Olivet will figure this out, right?"

"Demon, Dan. *De-mon!*"

"Yeah, I know, Squirt. I saw it too, remember?" He sighs. "We can't freak out. We have to be ready if it shows up again. So, let's focus on getting through the next couple hours till the doc calls back. Can you do that for me?"

I nod. Not like I have much of a choice in the matter. Freak out or try to stay on the up and up, ready to pounce if the thing comes back.

"Up for a horror movie marathon on Chiller?" Dan tries to be funny.

"*Really, Officer Dan?*"

He shrugs and tosses me the remote. Neither of us will be getting much sleep tonight, I'm thinking, so I settle for something I know will cause Dan to groan in sheer horror…a *Twilight* marathon!

Sure enough, as soon as he sees it, he tries to steal the remote. Nope, he's gonna suffer for making me miss out on the best burger in town, even if I have to suffer through it too.

Chapter Five

My teeth are chattering, and I can't get warm. Fuzz greets my eyes when I blink them open. The TV. The screen has gone all snowy. Did one of us roll on the remote and change the channel? Dan has Direct TV, so the channels never go snowy unless you change the input. Dan is sprawled in his comfy chair, drool falling out of his mouth. I so want a camera right now. Wait…I can use my new phone to take a picture!

I struggle to sit up. My body feels like it's weighted down. I'd fallen asleep on the floor, so now my muscles are protesting the hard surface. It's freezing in here. That isn't helping my aching back, either. Note to self, never watch TV on Dan's floor again.

Once I'm up on my knees, I freeze. I'm eye level with the glasses we'd used for our pop earlier. Ice makes trails up the surfaces of the glasses, spidering here and there. I look around, but don't see any ghosts. That doesn't stop the creepy feeling, though. It's like someone is watching me. I don't like it.

The floorboards creak, and my head swivels in the direction of Dan's bedroom. He has a small apartment. It's basically a living room and kitchen combo, a bedroom, and a tiny, tiny bathroom. There are few places to hide in here. The satellite box tells me it's after midnight, which explains why it's so dark. We must have fallen asleep without turning on any lights.

I listen, but don't hear anything. Thoughts of that thing flood my memories, and I'm tempted to wake up Dan, but if it's only an ordinary ghost, I'd rather get it out before Officer Dan wakes up and freaks out about a ghost in his place. Decision made, I push myself up off the floor and take a hesitant step toward the closed bedroom door. I swear someone is watching me, but I shake it off. Can't show them any fear.

I am only a few inches from the door when I hear footsteps on the other side. They aren't loud, but he has carpet, if that makes a difference. My hand reaches for the door, but I hear footsteps behind me. I whirl, but see nothing. Someone is watching me, trying to scare me. Freaking ghosts.

"You can't scare me," I whisper, trying not to wake Dan. Ghosts don't have to make themselves seen. That's one of the first things I learned. Most show themselves to me because they want something, but they can hide too. This one is hiding. "Show yourself."

Floorboards creak on the other side of the bedroom door, and I turn back to it. The bedroom is carpeted. The floor shouldn't be creaking. I reach for the doorknob again, and a wave of icy cold hits me as soon as I touch it. It seeps into my bones, and I shudder, my teeth starting to chatter. The cold is the worst part. It invades my body and chases out any warmth. It's the cold of the dead, and it hurts.

The door opens easily, and a small gasp escapes me. The room beyond is a studio of some sort. There are paintings everywhere. Dark, morbid paintings. Images of tortured souls leap out of the canvases, their pain and horror evident in their eyes. I hear a scraping sound and look to the left. Someone is standing in front of a canvas, muttering to themselves. I take a step into the room, and chills begin to wrack my body. I'm so cold, but I have to see who it is. There's something about the painting he's working on that I have to see.

My legs feel weighted down worse than they were before. The cold is intense, and as I force myself forward, I see ice start to form on my fingers, spreading up my hands. I push on, the need to see that painting outweighing everything else. I have to see it.

The man has his back turned to me, but his unruly curls escape everywhere. They are dark like mine. He's holding a jar with dark red liquid in it. His brush dips into it then makes more strokes across the canvas. The floor around him is soaked with red paint. All the paintings in here are done in red paint.

A tinny smell hits me as I draw closer. It's a smell I recognize. It's blood. He's not using red paint, he's using blood. All the paintings are blood soaked. I can see it drip from his paintbrush. He's using blood to paint his portraits. Bile rises in my throat, but I swallow it down. I need to see what he's painting.

An image of a young woman stares at me, her eyes tortured. There is such a lost look in them. I feel her pain and despair. Her face is beautiful, hauntingly so, but it's her eyes that hold a person. They are the only other spark of color in the painting. Hazel eyes, much like my own, stare at me helplessly.

The man mutters again and stalks over to a table. He pulls back a sheet, and I want to scream. There's a woman strapped down to the table, and he uses a knife to open an old wound on her arm, letting blood drip down into his now empty jar. She moans softly, but doesn't move. I can see she's almost dead, and I want to shout, to scream for him to leave her alone, but I'm frozen. I can't move. It's the woman who he's painting, and she looks so familiar to me, but I don't know from where.

When he's collected enough blood, he throws the sheet back over her and comes back to the painting.

"It's beautiful, isn't it?" he asks me. *"Did you know the soul can be found in the blood?"*

"Who are you?" I ask.

"You have beautiful features," he says. *"You'd make a wonderful subject."*

Uh, no, not gonna happen, not in a billion gazillion years.

He turns around, and I try to take a step backward, but I can't. Ice has formed around my feet, locking them in place. So not good. He tilts his head, and his eyes are dark, an edge of madness in them. He comes to stand by me, and his fingers graze my cheek. I flinch from the cold, and he smiles.

"So beautiful," he whispers.

"Get away from me, freak!" I shout and struggle to make my feet move.

"You shouldn't talk to me like that, Emma Rose."

"What?" Why did he call me that? Does he think I'm someone else?

His eyes start to bleed black ooze like that thing from earlier, and I renew my efforts to get free. Is he a demon? Dang it, I hate the fear that crawls up my spine.

"Poor Emma Rose," he murmurs. *"You seek the truth, but you don't really want to know it."* He leans in, his breath putrid, smelling of rot. *"I can show you the truth, but are you willing to go as far as it takes to find out?"*

"What are you talking about?" I demand. Why does he keep calling me that? Is he some psycho ghost who's trapped in a nightmare and wants to trap me too?

"Let me show you, my Emma Rose, let me show you."

He takes my hand and pulls it toward him, the knife he had earlier coming up. He slices it across my wrist, and I watch in horror as blood wells up. He picks up another jar and lets my blood drip into it. Drop by drop it falls until there is a good inch in the jar. I can't struggle, try as I might. It feels like before, when that thing touched me. I'm paralyzed.

He dips the brush into my blood and starts to paint again. The image on the canvas begins to move, to breathe.

Black goo oozes from the canvas and drips onto the floor. The pool of liquid snakes its way toward me, and I can't move, my feet frozen. It reaches my sneakers and begins to crawl its way up my shoes and reaches the bare skin of my legs. Pain explodes everywhere.

I scream.

Chapter Six

"Mattie! Mattie, wake up!"

Someone is shaking me, and I come awake violently, my fist swinging. It connects with something solid, and I hear a muttered curse.

"Stop it, Mattie, it's me!"

Dan. It's Dan. Oh, God, did I just hit Dan? I blink my eyes open, and he's staring down at me in concern. I see the redness on his cheek and realize I whopped him a good one. "I'm so sorry!"

"What were you dreaming about?" he asks and helps me up off the floor. He frowns and grabs my hand. There's blood on it. Those big old brown eyes widen when he sees how badly my wrist is bleeding. He lets out a curse and runs to the kitchen.

I stare in shock and fascination at my wrist. There's a bloody gash going across it exactly where I'd been cut in my dream. I managed to carry the wound out of my dream? No way. No freaking way.

Dan is back, cleaning and binding the wound tightly. He's giving me covert looks of suspicion. Does he really think I'd cut my wrists? As if I'd ever be stupid enough to do that, no matter what situation I'm in. Idiot boy.

"You'd best get that idea right out of that head of yours," I tell him, the aggravation plain in my voice.

"Mattie…"

"Look, Officer Dan," I say sarcastically, "if I survived this long being plagued by ghosts, what makes you think I'd go and do this now?"

"Your mom."

Dang, why does he always have to have a good reason for everything? Thoughts of my mom freak me out beyond belief, but I still wouldn't do this.

"Dan, I didn't do this. Besides, you forget I'm religious. Just 'cause I don't go to church doesn't mean I don't believe in Heaven. Suicide is a sure way to buy yourself a one-way ticket on the train to down under. And I'm not that selfish, either," I add. Killing yourself might stop your problems at the moment, but it leaves everyone who cares about you in as much pain or more than you were in before you offed yourself.

"Then what happened, Squirt?"

I tell him about my dream, and his frown deepens. "You're sure it felt like that thing from before?"

"No, the man was definitely not like that thing, but the way I was frozen felt like what happened to me."

"I don't like this, Mattie, not one bit." He stands and starts to pace.

"Well, we knew ghosts could hurt people," I offer.

"Not when you're asleep!"

I wince. Dan is slightly more freaked out than usual because he saw that thing earlier. He doesn't understand why he could see it. He's as normal as normal can get. The idea of seeing something he didn't believe in only a few months ago has him on edge. Not that I blame him. Even though I've been seeing ghosts since I was five, this thing has me weirded out more than normal too.

My phone belts out the tunes of Fall Out Boy and causes both of us to jump. Dan reaches it before I can, and relief crosses his face.

"Doctor, hang on a sec and let me put you on speaker."

"Hey, Doc," I greet him once Dan puts the phone on the coffee table. "What took you so long? I thought you were calling back in a couple of hours."

"Sorry about that, kids."

Why does everyone insist on calling us kids? Dan is twenty, and I recently turned seventeen. Kids, we are not.

"I had to contact a friend of mine. Took me a couple hours to get him to answer his phone. He was on a hunt out in Arizona with his boys."

"And?" Dan prompts, leaning in close to the phone.

"Well, what you two saw was definitely a demon, but I don't know what kind. I need more information."

"Yeah, we figured that out already, Doc," I tell him. "Why did Dan see it?"

"Well, it might be a little hard to believe," he says hesitantly. He knows how un-supernatural Dan can be. If he doesn't see it with his own two eyes,

50

he doesn't believe it.

"According my friend, there's really only two types of beings that can see demons. One is someone like you, Mattie. Your essence is essentially that of a ghost, and you can see things on a plane of existence most of us can't. That thing exists outside this plane of reality, and therefore, you see it."

Makes sense, sorta. "And Dan?"

"Well, there's only one other type of being that can see them." The doc clears his throat. "Dan, what do you know about your family history?"

"Dan was adopted, Doc," I answer before Dan can. "He doesn't know anything about his birth parents."

There is a sigh on the other end of the line. "Do you know about the Knights Templar?"

"Weren't they some big secret society or something in the Dark Ages?" Dan asks. The frown creasing his forehead tells me he's working hard to remember.

"Or something," Doc says ruefully. "Not quite the Dark Ages either—actually quite a bit later. They came into being in the early twelfth century, during the First Crusade. They were many, many things and were granted a lot of power by the Church. One of their prime duties was to hunt down demons and other evil beings for the church. Most were trained exorcists."

"They could see demons?" I ask. "How, exactly?"

"It was in their blood, Mattie," Doc explains. "Or so the story tells us. In the Dark Ages, the Church was starting to become powerful, but there were issues. Demons, to be more specific. They had overrun the masses, invaded the Church, and many were beginning to lose their faith. The balance of power was tipped in the demons' favor because the only thing that could see them in their true form was an Angel. Now, Angels are busy creatures. They always have been, as they are God's warriors. So, to sway the balance of power back to the side of good, Angels granted some of the Church's most holy knights the ability to see demons."

Dan and I crowd around the phone, listening. Doc is a born storyteller.

"The Angels shared their blood with the knights, and when they woke up, the Knights Templar were born. They were able to see evil in its true forms. Demons are notorious for hiding in people. Humans offer them a way to walk in our plane of existence, and they love to cause holy hell here on Earth." He chuckles at what he must assume is a joke. "Anyway, the Knights were given the full backing of the Church, and within a decade, they had the demon infestation under control."

"Didn't the Church end up killing them off, though?" Dan frowns.

"You're getting ahead of the story, Dan," the doc tells him. "The Church utilized the Knights to gain the massive amount of power it was famous for back in the day. The Knights were also amassing power and learning to control their gifts. They started to delve into all sorts of things, from engineering to alchemy. They became a force the Church soon learned to fear because they couldn't control them anymore, and the Knights had abilities that terrified the Church. They soon saw them as abominations rather than the saviors they were. All of this came about because of a little demon whispering in the Pope's ear. Or so the story says."

"What happened?" I ask. If Doc was my history teacher, I don't think I'd ever fall asleep.

"On Friday, October 13, 1307, King Phillip, the King of France, ordered the Knights arrested, stating that, 'God is not pleased. We have enemies of the faith in the kingdom.'"

"These were the same people who had just saved their butts?" I shake my head.

"Yes, unfortunately so, Mattie." Doc sighs. "Many were killed, some even burned at the stake for witchcraft because of what they could do. What was left of the order went into hiding. The Freemasons were rumored to be what was left of the Knights Templar in later history. I can tell you what I know to be true about the surviving members of the Knights. They couldn't simply turn their backs on who they were, what God had blessed them to do. They were hunters, and that is what they continued to do. Their numbers have dwindled over the years, and many have lost a lot of the gifts that were dominant in their bloodlines in the past, but they persevere and continue to fight demons and other evils."

"Hold up a second, here, Doc," I interrupt. I think I know where he's going with this, and Dan is not going to be receptive. "Are you saying Dan is a descendant of one of these Knight people, and that's why he could see the demon? Why can't he see my ghosts, then?"

"That's simple, Mattie. Knights were created to see evil and destroy it. Your ghosts, up until now, haven't been evil. They've been lost souls looking for help. Dan hasn't been able to see them because of that."

"You can't really expect me to believe that," Dan scoffs. I can see the terror in his eyes, though. He's seriously spooked. "I am not...not some freak of nature."

"Oh, so, I'm a freak because I can see ghosts?" I ask, hurt.

His eyes soften. "No, that's not what I meant, Mattie..."

"That's what it sounded like."

He sighs and runs a hand through his hair. He is good and truly freaked. He's pacing, and he keeps flexing his fingers—his tell, if you will. I learned to pick up on it when we played poker.

"You grew up seeing ghosts," he says after a minute. "It's normal for you. Then I see a...a demon, and the doctor tells me it's because I'm a long-lost descendent of Angels? It's a hard pill to swallow, Mattie. You go to church and believe in all that. I don't. My parents never went to church. I didn't grow up believing in Angels and demons, or even ghosts, for that matter. I was raised that the only real evil in the world is in the form of humanity. That's not who I am."

"Doesn't matter if you believe in God or not, Officer Dan," I say softly. "He believes in you."

"Mattie..." The warning is clear in his voice. Best not to push him too hard right now. He's overwhelmed and not coping very well.

"Well, think about this. Your compulsion to help people might come from your ancestors," I tell him. "You have wicked skills as a police officer. So, maybe it follows that you were born to find evil and fight it."

"No, that's *not* what I do now," he denies hotly. "I'm a rookie cop who walks a beat."

"Dan, your captain wouldn't have sent you to Quantico for training with the Behavior Analysis Unit if she didn't think you were going to be a great cop."

"I'm studying forensics," he counters. "I won't be on the streets after I get my degree. I'll be working behind the scenes to help the detectives."

"No, you won't," I tell him. "You're a good cop, Dan. It's who you are. You'd never be happy puttering around in a lab examining lint, and you know it! You'd want to be out there looking for clues, interviewing witnesses, and working to solve the mystery."

"Kids…"

"*We're not kids!*" we both yell, and I can almost see the doc wincing. He's gotten between some of our fights before. It's never pretty.

"Sorry," he mutters. "What I wanted to say is that it's only one theory. Dan can mull it over, and I'll keep looking for more answers."

"Or," I say sweetly, "Dan can stop being pig-headed and accept the fact that he's Angel Boy."

"Mattie…that is not…you…" Dan sputters, unable to finish his sentence. He obviously hates that nickname. I likey.

"Mattie!" Doc's tone is very sharp. "Stop teasing him. Did Dan tease you when you told him about your gift?"

Dang it. Why did he have to go and remind me of that? The doc just took all the fun out of it.

"Fine," I mutter. "I won't tease him. Great way to suck all the fun out of this, Doc."

Doc sighs. I can tell he is not amused. "It's late, and I know you guys probably need to get to sleep…"

"Wait," Dan interrupts, and he tells him about my dream. "When she woke up, her wrist was bleeding all over my white carpet."

So not my fault his carpet is stained.

"You mean she physically manifested a wound she received in a dream?" Doc asks, his voice extremely worried. That can't be at all good if the Spook Doctor is spooked.

"Yeah." Dan sighs. "I guess that means we should be worried?"

"You should probably be cautious," he says slowly. "What she experienced is very uncommon, but coupled with the demon stalking her, I wouldn't take any chances. I'll be in New Orleans tomorrow and will make sure I get her a protection charm."

My eyes narrow. "Doc, I am *not* wearing chicken feet around my neck."

He laughs outright. "Oh, my girl, you shouldn't watch so much TV. Most gris-gris are not made of chicken feet. Most have herbs in them."

"I don't do Voodoo, Doc."

"If you want to stay safe, you will, Mattie Louise," he tells me matter-of-factly. "No arguments. I'll overnight it to you as soon as it's ready, and I don't want you to take it off."

"I'm not going to be here," I tell him. "Meg is taking me somewhere for my birthday."

"Where's she taking you?" he asks.

"Not sure." I shrug. "It's a surprise."

"Will Dan be with you?"

"Uh, I don't think so?" I look at Dan questioningly.

"I have to go to New Orleans myself first," he tells Doc. "I can pick it up then deliver it in person."

He knows where she's taking me, and he's been holding out? I give him an outraged look, and he winks. At least some of the shock is wearing off if he can wink.

"Good," Doc says, relieved. "Mattie, I need to do some more research on your transference dream, but I'll get back to you within a day or so, I promise. I have a lot to do the next few days. We're investigating a very haunted house, one that has terrorized its occupants for over a hundred and fifty years."

"No worries, Doc," I tell him. "You take your time while I torture Angel Boy here into telling me where Meg is taking me tomorrow."

Dan growls, the doc sighs, and I hang up on him

"Now, Officer Dan, where am I going?"

I can see by the stubborn set of his jaw, this is going to take a while. I flip the *Twilight* reruns back on and quirk my eyebrow. He wants to torture me, I'll torture him.

It's going to be a long night.

Chapter Seven

I ignore the constant pounding on the bathroom door. Dan is being impatient. We have plenty of time to get to the airport. I'm in no hurry to board the death trap. I can so imagine surviving the plane crash and being bombarded by the ghosts of the mangled passengers...I have enough to deal with without that complication, thank you very much.

Speaking of complications, I glance down at the white bandage on my wrist. It's glaringly obvious what it is, at least to me. If Meg has half a brain cell—which she does, unfortunately—she'll start bugging me with questions the minute she zeros in on it. I'm supposed to leave my bandages off my hands periodically, but seeing the wrapping on my wrist, I think I'll opt for putting them back on. It's too hot outside to wear long sleeves. Weatherman said it's going to be over 100 today, with a heat index of about 115. This way I can at least hide the bandage on my wrist.

"Mattie! We still have to swing by your place and get your bags!" Dan yells through the door. "Or did you forget about that?"

I sigh. No, I haven't forgotten that fact. I'm still wearing my clothes from yesterday. I just don't want to hurry to the airport and the possibility of my death. There are very few things that scare me, but planes do. Face it, being up in the air thousands of feet above the ground, if one of those engines malfunctions…I shudder at the thought.

"Dan, it's six-thirty in the morning! We have plenty of time."

"No, we don't," he shouts through the door. "Meg has already texted me five times. Your flight boards at nine, which means you need to be through security before eight-thirty. It can take an hour just to get through TSA."

Did he say Meg *texted* him? I rip open the door and stalk out into the hallway. Dan is staring at me with a frown. "When did you two start texting?" I demand.

He looks slightly embarrassed, as well he should, since he almost kissed me yesterday. Texting my best friend?

"She demanded I keep her updated when you went missing," he says slowly. "We've sorta been talking since then."

Fury runs through me unlike anything I have ever known. I want to hit him and Meg in that minute. I'm so angry I go back into the bathroom and slam the door in his face.

"Don't get mad, Squirt," he calls.

Don't get mad? *Don't get mad?* Oh, the nerve. "She's too young for you!"

"She's eighteen, Mattie."

That feels like a sucker punch to the gut. So, because she's a year older than I am, and prettier, and rich…and…ohhhh. I want to scream.

I open the bathroom door and stomp to the kitchen. I pick up Dan's phone, which he conveniently left on the kitchen island, and dial Meg's number.

"Dan?" She picks up on the first ring. "Are you guys on your way yet?"

"No, we are not on our way, Megan, and nor are we going to be!" I hang up and dial Mary's number. It goes to voicemail, dang it.

"Mary, it's Mattie. Can you pick me up at Dan's, please? Call me back, and I'll give you the address."

I throw his phone down and storm past him into the bathroom, slamming the door behind me and locking it.

Dan's phone rings, and I hear him talking softly. After a minute, he knocks on the door. I ignore him. I can wait in here until Mary comes to get me.

He knows I don't trust people very easily, and here he goes flirting with my best friend behind my back. I'm doing my best to hold on to the anger, because if I let it go, I'm going to hurt. The truth is, I guess maybe I do love Dan more than just a friend or a brother. I love him a lot, and this proves to me how badly he can hurt me.

"Mattie, open the door, please."

"Go away!" I shout.

I can hear him sigh through the door. "Meg wants to talk to you."

"Well, I don't want to talk to either one of you!"

Just yesterday I was thinking what a great friend she was for not going after Dan because I might like him. I can't believe I didn't see it. Dan has softened me up too much. I can't wait to graduate and get away from everybody. Maybe I should look into the whole emancipation thing and transfer to a school out in California. It would be warm, and I wouldn't have to deal with back-stabbing friends.

"Mattie, you're being a brat about this," Dan says, frustrated. "It's not like we planned for this to happen, it just did."

Planned for this to happen? "Are you two dating?"

"Yes."

I slide down the wall, unable to breathe for a second. Pain goes straight through me. They were dating and hiding it from me? How could they do this to me?

I pull out my phone and call Dan's dad. It's one of the contacts Dan had pre-stored in it. I ask him to come get me, and he agrees.

"Mattie? Who are you talking to?"

I don't answer. I can't. The minutes tick by, and I can hear Dan talking to someone on the phone, probably either Meg or his dad. Great. Now, I'll have to play twenty questions once his dad gets here. I want to hide out under my covers and cry like a girl. Instead, I call the only other person who means anything to me. I call Dr. Olivet.

He picks up on the first ring. "Mattie? What's wrong? Did something else happen?"

"Doc, I need a favor."

"If I can, you know I will."

61

"Do you want a real live ghost girl with you on your hunt?"

There's a long pause. I can almost see him trying to figure out what my angle is.

"Mattie, I'd love to have you here with me, but aren't you going away with your friend for the week?"

"Not anymore," I say bitterly. Friends don't go behind your back and steal the guy who means more to you than anyone else ever has. "Do you want my help or not?"

"Of course, Mattie. I'll call you back with the time of the flight. When you get to the airport, print off the ticket, and I'll have someone pick you up when you land if I can't."

"Thanks, Doc." I don't even bother to say bye, hanging up the phone. Now I just need to wait for Dan's dad to get here to take me to Jane's. I can get Mary to pick me up and take me to the airport. I'll even leave the room purple if she can keep Dan and Meg away from me until I leave.

"Mattie, if you don't open this door, I swear I'm going to break it down!"

There's a hint of panic in Dan's voice. I think deep down he might still be afraid I actually did try to cut my wrist. Stupid. He should know me better than that.

"Go ahead and lose your security deposit." It would serve him right.

"Please open the door, Mattie."

The doorbell rings, and I hear it open and close. There's a muffled conversation, and then footsteps lead back to the bathroom door.

"Mattie?"

I close my eyes. Meg is here? Freaking fabulous.

"Go away, Megan."

"No, I won't go away, Mattie," she says. "We're friends..."

"Friends?" I shout and jump up, unlocking the door and yanking it open. "Friends? Don't you dare call yourself my friend anymore."

"Mattie, we didn't want you to find out like this..."

"Do you know I thought I was lucky to have found a friend like you? Me, the foster kid who's never had real friends or family, finally found people I could trust, people who cared about me."

"I *do* care about you."

I slap her, and she stumbles back. Dan catches her before she falls.

"Don't," I warn her. "If you were my friend, you would never have gone after him. You told me you wouldn't until I figured out how I felt. You lied to me, Megan. You broke my trust. *Both* of you did."

There's another knock at the door. Dan frowns when he sees his dad standing in the doorway, looking confused and concerned as he stares at the three of us.

"Thanks for coming to get me, Mr. Richards," I say, trying to keep my voice even and steady.

"Honey, what's wrong?" he asks.

"Nothing's wrong, I just need a ride home." I can see he doesn't believe a word of it. He looks at Dan, who looks at the floor. Mr. Richards's frown deepens. "Can we go?"

He nods. I step around the backstabbers and

attempt to leave with a little dignity.

"Mattie, I know you're upset..." My back stiffens at the tameness of that word. "Call me when you calm down, okay?" Dan pleads.

I pull the phone he'd given me out of my pocket. I really, really like this phone, but I throw it at his head. "No, *Officer Dan*. I don't think I'll be calling you. Keep your phone."

"Mattie, you need that phone. That's why I got it for you..."

"I don't want anything from you!" I hiss and march out the door, down the stairs, and wait for Mr. Richards beside his Lexus. Lord knows how long it's gonna take him to come downstairs. He'll probably grill Dan first.

Now I need to get through the rest of the day without breaking down.

I can do it.

I can.

Chapter Eight

I can't, I can't, I can't!

I feel closed in, sweat rolls down my back, and I have the sudden urge to hurl. The airplane isn't loud, but I can feel the dip as we start to dive down to land. What if the landing gear doesn't release? What if an engine goes out? Please, please don't blow up.

Up until this point, I've been semi-fine. Mary loaned me her iPod, and I've distracted myself by listening to music I normally wouldn't touch. She and I have very dissimilar tastes in music. I won't be borrowing it again, but I needed something to take my mind off the death trap I was in and to try to block out thoughts of Dan and Meg.

It's still hard to believe what they did. I mean, I know I didn't have any real claim to him, and I wasn't old enough until today to even think about it, but still, you don't do that. It's part of the unwritten code of best friends. You don't touch another girl's guy, even if they aren't together.

God bless Mary, though. Once she found out

what happened, she went into bulldog mode. Neither Dan nor Meg ever got near me. Both of them showed up at Mary's, wanting to see me, and she told them both where to go in no uncertain terms. By the time she was done, even my ears were ringing. Mary's good people, and I'm lucky to have her. We went through a lot together, and I know no matter what, she'll never betray me. She's family.

But so is Dan. I don't know if I can forgive him, though. Once you break my trust, I never give it back. He and I might end up losing everything we've built, but he will always be my family. That much I know is true. It's weird, and I couldn't explain it to Mary very well, either. Probably because I can't even explain it to myself.

Deep down, I think I decided to come to New Orleans to test him. If he really cares, and he meant what he said about never letting me push him away, he'll come find me. He's supposed to be here anyway to check out what the PI found out about my mom. If I mean more to him than Meg does, he'll come find me. I hope.

The plane jolts as we touch down on the runway, and I let out a breath I didn't know I was holding. Thank you, God. I send up my prayers and take a deep breath. I survived my first plane ride.

The heat slaps me in the face as soon as I get near the exit door of the plane. Great, I came from one heat box right into another one. *Suck it up, Mattie*, I tell myself. Better here than listening to Meg and Dan try to explain themselves.

Not that the heat bothers me for more than a second. I am surrounded by cold seconds after I step foot on the tarmac. I want to run right back on the plane. Whispers bombard me, so loud they are deafening. I can't even make out what any of them are saying. It makes me dizzy, and I stumble. Someone catches me and asks if I'm okay. I think I mumble a yes and manage to stagger inside. How could I forget that New Orleans is the city of the dead? I shouldn't be here.

I only packed one carry on. Finding it, I push through the mass of people fighting to get downstairs to the baggage claim area. Everywhere, the ghosts are everywhere. The need to scream at them to go away claws at my throat. My eyes water from the pain exploding in my head from the magnitude of ghosts whispering to me. Their emotions crowd into me, and I want to curl up and cry. So much pain and anger.

"Mattie Hathaway?"

I hear my name called and look up through blurry eyes. There's a guy standing about twenty feet from me with my name held up on piece of paper. I blink, clearing the moisture from my eyes. He's tall, really tall, probably well over six feet. And muscular. Maybe a bit too muscular for me, though. His brown eyes are warm and full of concern. They remind me so much of Dan's in that moment, tears threaten. I have to forcefully remind myself I do *not* cry. I refuse to do it. I've shed enough tears over that boy in the last twenty-four hours to last a lifetime. No more.

"Yeah?" I ask, trying to stay focused on him and drown out the voices smothering me.

"I'm Caleb Malone. Dr. Olivet sent me to pick

you up." His voice is as warm as his eyes. He fishes his phone out of his pocket and hands it to me. "He said you'd want to call him."

He's right about that. No way am I getting into a car with some strange guy without verifying who he is. That's how girls get raped and killed.

"Hey, Doc," I say when he answers. "Just checking to make sure Muscles here is the guy you sent."

Dr. Olivet laughs at my comment. "Yes, Mattie, Caleb is who I sent to pick you up. How are you feeling?"

By the eagerness in his voice, I'm guessing he knows how badly I'm being affected by the ghosts here in the city. I can see them streaming toward me from all corners.

"Doc, you and I have to have a chat about your eagerness when it comes to ghosts."

He chuckles. "I'll see you soon, Mattie, and thanks for coming down. I know you hate talking about your gift, let alone letting anyone see you when you use it."

My eyes widen. I'd completely zoned that out. No one knows what I can do outside the Doc and Dan. I never let anyone see it. I'm not that kid, the weirdo everyone laughs at. I've worked too hard to hide this from everyone.

"Um, Doc, about that, can we please keep it between you and me?"

He's very quiet, and I get the distinct impression he might have already spilled the beans. Dang it!

"We'll talk about it when you get here," he says. "Can you put Caleb on the phone, please?"

I hand the phone over and glower at everyone around me. Freaking great. Now they all know what a freak show I am.

"Ready?" Caleb asks and attempts to take my carry on.

"I got it." I wave him off. I can roll my own bag. Besides, I need it keep myself from falling. The ghosts really are affecting me more than I can handle right now. It hurts. I follow him outside, and we board one of the shuttle buses that takes us to the east parking deck. Caleb drives a beat-up Ford pickup like Dan, only Caleb's F150 is huge compared to Myrtle.

I stow my carry on in the bed of the truck then climb in. The seat is cloth and very, very comfy, like it's seen a lot of wear over the years. Caleb turns the air on full blast, making me shiver even more. The oppressive heat outside actually helped me warm up a bit, but now I'm back to freezing.

"Hey, do you mind if we cut the air down?" I ask after about twenty minutes. I'd love to turn the heat on, but I don't want him thinking I'm weirder than he probably already does.

He smiles, and I blink, seeing Dan for a second. It's the jaw, I realize. His facial structure is so much like Dan's, it's amazing. They could be brothers.

"I'll do you one better." Instead of turning the air down, he flips it to the heat and leaves it on full blast. "You're not the only one who gets cold when they come around."

My head whips around, and I stare at him. Does he mean what I think he means?

He grins at me. "Yeah, I see ghosts too. How are

you holding up? I know the first time I came to New Orleans, the pain got so bad I passed out for a couple days. Freaked my parents out like nothing else."

He was a reaper too?

"My brothers and my sister can see them too," he continues, ignoring my mouth-hitting-my-chin moment. "From what the doc said, you're a little different from us, though."

"Different?"

"We really only see the bad ones, the ones who have gone vengeful, and you see the good ones as well as the bad ones. He told us you were supposed to be a reaper or something."

Doc had been very busy blabbing my secrets to all. I purse my lips at the thought. He and I are so gonna have a chat when I see him.

"I don't think I've ever seen him this excited," Caleb says. "He's like a kid at Christmas."

"Is the house really haunted?" I ask, keeping my voice low. My head is killing me. I'd sell an organ right about now if someone offered me some Motrin.

Caleb sighs. "I don't know. We haven't seen anything, but then you know ghosts only show themselves if they want to be seen."

"But don't you feel them?" I ask, shivering as more of them crowd into the truck. I close my eyes to keep from seeing the mutilated corpses, bloated flesh, and hollow eyes begging me to help them.

"Sometimes I get cold," he says with a nod. "Like right now, I feel like we're knee-deep in snow in an arctic blast. I'd guess there are a couple of them with us right now?"

I nod. "More than a couple," I say. "Hundreds of them."

My hand shakes as I raise it to push my hair out of my face. The pain is starting to get worse, and my vision is blurring again.

"Mattie?" Caleb's voice is full of worry.

"Yeah?"

"Your nose is bleeding."

I touch the area between my lip and nose, and my fingers come away bloody. Oh, this is so not good. Black spots start to appear, and the voices scream at me, stabbing into my head one after another. It feels like someone is drilling away at my skull while someone else gleefully stabs my brain with an ice pick.

"Hurts," I whisper. I'm down to one-word sentences.

"Dad'll know what to do," Caleb tells me. "Don't worry, Mattie. You're gonna be okay."

I don't think so, but instead of stating the obvious, I concentrate on not passing out. The truck picks up speed, and I can't even pay attention to the gorgeous scenery I know is flying by us.

The farther we drive, the more intense the pain becomes. They're screaming something at me. I can feel the fear pulsing in waves around me. We turn off the main highway onto a dirt road. The pounding in my head worsens, and as we drive up to an old plantation home, I finally understand something. The fear they are giving off is fear for me. They are trying to warn me not to go into the house.

Apryl Baker

"Mattie, are you ready to go inside?" Caleb asks as he parks the truck in front of the steps.

"Yeah," I pant, my breath coming in short gasps. The ghosts are doing their best to warn me, but they're hurting me. "Please stop shouting," I whisper. "It hurts."

"I'm not shouting." Caleb frowns.

"Not you." I open the passenger side door. My feet hit the ground a moment later, and I catch hold of the door to keep from falling. I squint and look up at the old plantation home with its beautiful columns. I gasp as I feel the darkness emanating from it. It surrounds me, and the ghosts wail in terror.

The pain behind my eyes intensifies, and I see something standing on the porch. It's hazy at first, but I can feel it. It's daring me to come inside. That thing wants me in there. I've never come across a ghost like this. It's full of hate and rage, but it *is* a ghost. It's not like the demon thing from before. This is a ghost, but one unlike any I've ever come across.

I try to take a step, and pain lances through my head, causing me to stumble. I feel the blackness coming, and as much as I try to fight it, I can't. I don't want to go into that house.

It's a bad, bad place full of bad things.

Chapter Nine

"I'm not sure that's a good idea," I hear. My eyes are too heavy to open. Pain surrounds me. I feel like I've just been ten rounds with a bulldog, and the bulldog won.

"It's the only thing I know that can block the whispers," another deep voice speaks up.

"James, will that interfere with her gift, with what she can do? She's not like you and the boys. Her gift is different." That's the doc. I'd know his voice anywhere. What are they talking about?

"I don't know, Doc." I can hear frustration in the man's voice. "We have to do something, though, and this is the only thing I know that will work. If we wait too much longer, she might hemorrhage."

What? Hemorrhage? Then I remember my nosebleed. Is that what he means? Just freaking great. Survive a serial killer, only to die because ghosts were trying to help me but ended up hurting me.

"Here, Dad, what about this?" Caleb, maybe? "If we change the design a bit, it might help her to control it without losing her ability. I did draw it right, yeah?"

"That's not bad, Caleb," the man says, pride in his voice. "This could work. We can always go back to the original design if her condition doesn't improve."

My condition? I manage to force my eyes to open a small crack, only to be met by a blinding light. Pains stabs through my head again. It's too much, and I feel myself getting sucked back into the black hole of nothingness.

The next time I drag myself back to consciousness, it's utterly quiet. I strain my ears but hear nothing. My head isn't exploding anymore, either. The cold is intense, but bearable, and the whispers sound muted, not screaming full throttle.

I try to open my eyes and find that I can. The room is dark, so I can't really make out anything, but I'm glad I can do it without my entire being lighting up with shockwaves of pain. *Deep breaths*, I tell myself, and push up to a sitting position. The world doesn't tilt, and it's a good sign. I listen again, trying to hear the ghosts talking. They're muted. What in the world did Caleb and his dad do to me? Not that I'm complaining, mind you, but it's weird not to be able to hear them in full Technicolor. It's like an old black and white movie; the sounds are fuzzy, but you can almost make out what they're saying.

The need for a bathroom motivates me, and I swing my legs over the bed and wince at a sharp pain in my lower back. My hand finds the spot, and it's downright sore. I definitely need a mirror.

A small groan escapes as I stand. I swear I feel like I've taken a serious beatdown. Last time I felt like this was back in third grade when the school bully decided he wanted my lunch money, but I wanted it every bit as much. We'd ended up rolling around, and I got the snot beat out of me. It's a memory that sticks with me because not long after that I started to learn to defend myself.

I have seriously got to stop letting my emotions dictate my actions. If I hadn't run from Dan and Meg and my own hurt feelings, I wouldn't be in this situation right now. I could have been sitting home with Mary, eating a tub of ice cream and watching sappy movies. She'd have loved it, and I would have been miserable, but at least I would have been safe. I don't feel so safe right now.

This house makes me nervous and edgy. I feel like I'm being watched, and the house itself is riddled with ghosts. Most seem afraid, as none of them have shown themselves to me except for the one on the porch, but I can feel them all. Some are afraid, some feel lonely, but there are just as many that are angry and want to lash out. It's those I'm worried about. I know firsthand that ghosts can cause a person serious harm when they want to.

More than anything, though, I'm worried about the ghost I'd seen earlier, the one who'd wanted me in this house. I don't know why he did, but it can't be a good thing. That ghost isn't interested in crossing over. He wants something from me, and I can bet it's not something I'm willing to give.

I stub my toe against something hard and hop around on one foot for a second. Where's the danged light switch? My hand finds the wall, and I make my way slowly toward the sliver of light I see under what I'm assuming is the door. Man, I need to pee. A hand grabs me as I reach the doorknob and hauls me backward. Something like electricity shoots through me when his fingers wrap around my arm. Reacting on instinct, I go limp, and the hand loosens enough for me to turn and kick as hard as I can. I'm pretty sure I connected with his leg, but it's not enough for him to let me go. My eyes are finally adjusting to the darkness, and I can make out the basic outline of his shape. He's much bigger than I am, which means I have to play smart here. My hands are pretty useless since the attack, so I have to rely on my feet. I twist and try to land another blow, aiming for what I hope is his knees.

He jerks backward, narrowly avoiding my foot, but then he yanks me against him, and in trying to get away, we both end up falling on the floor. After a few rolls, I'm pinned to the floor and seething mad.

"Will you stop?" he hisses, his face close to mine.

Instead of answering, I do exactly what I was taught to do. I head butt him as hard as I can. Pain explodes in my own head, but he loosens his grip enough for me to throw him off and jump on his back. I grab a fistful of his hair and slam his face against the floor several times. He's cussing up a storm all the while. I grab his forearm and force it behind his back and up, exerting exactly the right amount of pressure. If he moves, he'll snap his arm.

Gotcha.

The door slams open, and light floods the room. I don't glance back. Even the slightest hesitation on my part could cause me to loosen my grip enough for him to get away.

"Mattie, what are you doing?" Dr. Olivet asks, his voice incredulous.

"This guy attacked me," I say and pull on his arm a little harder.

"Eli attacked you?" Caleb comes into my line of sight.

"No, I did *not* attack her," the guy beneath me snarls. "I was trying to help her."

"You were not! You grabbed my arm and…"

"And nothing," he growls. "I was trying to get your attention so you didn't kill yourself in the dark."

"Then you should have said something instead of grabbing me!"

"As funny as this all is, Mattie, do you think you could let my son up before you break his arm?"

I know that voice. I remember it from before. He was the one who was trying to help me. Caleb's dad?

Caleb reaches a hand down to me, and I take it, releasing my hold on his brother's arm and letting Caleb pull me up. Eli slowly gets to his feet and settles gorgeous aqua eyes on me. They are spitting mad. My breath catches a little when I take in his face. Good Lord, I've never in my life thought of a boy as beautiful, but this one is. He's tall, as tall as Caleb, but his hair is lighter than his brother's. It's a dark brown, but it's streaked with caramel highlights, giving it a lighter appearance. His complexion is darker, a golden color, compared to Caleb's softer tones. High cheekbones speak of an Indian heritage, and a day's worth of facial hair makes his face rugged and soft. Full lips make me want to see how soft they'd feel against mine.

It's his eyes, though, that I can't look away from. His eyes remind me of one of the few things I love. They are like the ocean right at daybreak, when the waves are soft and the foam rushes the sand. I've never seen anyone with eyes that color.

"Dude, you got your ass kicked by a girl." Caleb laughs, not even trying to conceal his smirk.

Eli lunges at his brother, but his dad catches him before he can move three inches. "Caleb, don't antagonize your brother. I'm sure he didn't expect her to come out swinging." There's a grin on their dad's face, and fortunately, Eli doesn't see it because he's still glaring menacingly at me and Caleb.

"Wouldn't dream of it, Dad," Caleb grins.

Dr. Olivet sighs. "Mattie, how are you feeling? Is your head still hurting?"

"I'm okay," I tell him. "Um, Doc, where's the bathroom? I really need to find one."

"I'll show you."

I step away from Caleb and make a wide berth around Eli to follow Doc down the hall. The bathroom is only three doors down from my room, and it's absolutely gorgeous. The room is all white with gold accents, but I don't mind that. The old-fashioned tub calls my name. It's huge and deep. The toilet is modern, but everything else in the room screams 19th century. The only splashes of color are the deep blue towels.

After taking care of my urgent need to pee, I rinse out my sewer mouth. Dear Lord, it tastes foul. How long have I been out? Now that I've taken care of my immediate needs, I don't really want to leave the bathroom. Truth be told, I'm a little embarrassed, something entirely new for me, but there it is. I grew up with the mentality of hit first before you get hit. Being a foster kid who lived in some really bad homes, I had to think like that. It gave me a bit of a reputation.

I lost my last boyfriend, Jake, because he saw me beat the snot out of his friend Tommy for threatening me. It disturbed him to know the rumors about me were true. It's one thing to hear about it, and another to see it live, up close, and personal. He was the first guy I ever dated who I thought might be able to look past all the shields I put up and see *me*. He did see the softer side most never bothered to get to know, but the first time he met the foster kid who doesn't take crap from anyone, he bailed. I mean, he didn't even officially break up with me. He just stopped talking to me. Not even a text or phone call when I was in the hospital recovering from Mrs. Olson's torture. It hurt a lot more than I liked to admit. I really, really liked Jake, but he couldn't handle the real Mattie Hathaway any more than the other guys.

I sigh and run my fingers through my hair. My curls are snarled and tangled. My face is pale, and the skin under my hazel eyes is bruised. I look awful. The past couple months have been rough on me. I've lost weight, and I've closed myself off more than usual. It's not healthy. Nancy wants me to see a psychologist, but I keep refusing. I don't do shrinks. I'll eventually get a handle on being tortured without any help. I will. Maybe if I say it enough, I'll even believe it.

Most nights, I can't convince myself of that, though. I wake up screaming, and I'm right back in that basement. I go on the offensive when I'm scared. I lashed out at everyone, even Dan. He stuck around, was there in the beginning every night when the nightmares terrorized me. I used to wake up in the hospital bed with him beside me, and I'd calm down almost instantly. I need him.

Being around Caleb and his dad makes me miss Dan. Heck, they even look like him. It could simply be me missing him and seeing him everywhere, but I don't think so. They all have the same brown eyes and chocolate hair, the same facial structure, and Caleb even sounds like Dan when he laughs. It's a little freaky. Eli, on the other hand, looks nothing like his family. Must take after their mother.

Eli...I don't want to think about him. He's another reason I want to hide in the bathroom. I had a strange reaction to him. I've never touched someone and felt electricity run through me before. It was the oddest feeling, like my body tensed up, and every nerve in it snapped. If I were still talking to Meg, I'd ask her about it. She seems much more boy-savvy than I am, even though I know for a fact I've had more boyfriends than she has. I'm still a virgin, though, and she's not. She would know what my reaction to him means.

I laugh bitterly. Meg betrayed me worse than

Dan did. Dan never promised to stay away from her, but Meg did, and she went after him anyway. Here I am, wanting advice from someone who didn't think twice about lying to my face. I need to start acting like the old Mattie again, the one who never let anyone in, who never got hurt. I don't like this new person who has feelings.

Stop it. I need to pull it together. Sitting in here hiding is not something Mattie Hathaway would ever do, at least not the old Mattie. Time to start acting like me again. Taking a deep breath, I square my shoulders and walk out to face everyone.

Chapter Ten

They're still in my room, or at least I assume it's my room because I woke up there. I can hear them talking softly and stop to eavesdrop.

"Mattie is unique," Dr. Olivet tells them. "She grew up in one foster home after another. That's why she is the way she is. She had to learn to defend herself."

"Her parents ditch her?" Eli asks.

It's a long moment before the doc answers. I think he's debating how to answer. He knows how private I am, but again, he needs them to understand if we are going to work together.

"Do you remember me telling you that Mattie is different from you?"

I hear a murmur.

"In order for Mattie to be able to do what she does, she had to die and be brought back. When she was little, her mother tried to kill her. Mattie died for only a few minutes, but it was long enough for her gift to activate."

"Her mother tried to kill her?" Caleb asks,

shocked.

"No wonder she's the way she is," their dad says softly. "What about her father?"

"She doesn't know who he is," Doc replies. "I know her friend Dan is looking into her past to try to find her father for her."

"Is that the same Dan she was talking about in her sleep?" Eli asks.

Oh, my God! I was talking in my sleep? What did I say? No, no, no...this isn't good.

"Yes," Doc agrees. "They seem to be in a bit of an argument at the moment."

"Sounded to me like he broke her heart," Caleb says. "I was tempted to find him and break his face."

I must have said some really personal stuff. My face has to be six shades of crimson right now.

"Really, Caleb?" Eli scoffs. "You've spoken to her for what, an hour, at best?"

Caleb sighs. "It's weird, but she's...I don't know how to explain it."

"Caleb's right," their dad agrees. "I didn't even speak to her, but I felt this sudden need to protect her. It gets stronger every time I'm near her. I think it's because she looks a little like Amelia."

Amelia? Who's Amelia?

"You're both crazy." Eli laughs. "I have no urge to do anything when it comes to that she-cat, except stay out of her way."

"You're just pissed because she gave you the smackdown!"

That's a new voice, a little boy.

"Shut up, Benny!" Eli grouches. "I did not get a

smackdown."

"So, you don't have a busted lip, black eye, and your forehead isn't bleeding?"

"Benny, don't antagonize your brother," their dad says while trying not to laugh. "He can't help the fact a girl beat him up."

"She did not...she..." I hear the growl emanating from him and chuckle. He really is upset and trying to play it off as nothing.

"At least you got beat down by a pretty girl," Benny says solemnly.

"Pretty?" Eli laughs harshly. "I don't..."

I push open the door, cutting him off. I have no need to hear him talk about me after seeing myself in the mirror. I look like an extra out of a zombie flick right now.

Five sets of eyes settle on me, and I want to squirm. They all look concerned, except for Eli. He looks pissed. I have no idea why I even care what he thinks, anyway.

"Hello, Mattie," the boys' dad smiles at me. "I'm James Malone, and these are my sons, Eli, Caleb, and Benjamin."

"Hi." Benny smiles shyly up at me.

"Hi." I grin back at him. He's as cute as a button and can't be more than seven or eight. He looks like Caleb, but he has Eli's eyes. I could just pinch his cheeks, he's so cute. "I'm Mattie."

"You're pretty."

"And you are working on being a heartbreaker." I laugh and ruffle his soft hair.

"How are you, Mattie?" Doc asks. "Can you still hear the ghosts, or are they completely gone?"

"It's weird," I say hesitantly, looking down at the floor. This isn't something I'm used to talking about around strangers. "It's like I can almost hear what they're saying, but the volume is turned down so low I can't make it out."

"It worked, then." James sighs, relieved. "We weren't sure you'd still be able to hear them."

"What did you do?" I ask curiously.

"I gave you a tattoo," Eli says, a wicked grin on his face.

"A tattoo?" My hand immediately goes to the small of my back where it's sore. I'd forgotten to check it in the bathroom.

"Eli inked you," Caleb says, "but I designed it. It's an old Druid protection spell that I changed a little so you could still hear them, but they wouldn't be able to overwhelm you."

"Druid protection spell?" Even I can hear the disbelief in my voice. Come on, really? Magic? Magic isn't real. Well, I'll give Criss Angel the benefit of the doubt. Some of the stuff he can do…

"It's designed to help you gain control over your abilities," Mr. Malone says. "The voices will come back louder and louder as you learn to mute them yourself. The only design I knew would have completely stripped you of your abilities, but you were bleeding out, and I was a little desperate. Caleb convinced me to try his design first before we did something so drastic. He's very good at drawing them. He saved your abilities."

I'm not sure I want him to have saved them. Not to be able to see and hear ghosts at every corner would have been a blessing. I could have been normal. I turn a glare upon the guy in question and he steps back from the vehemence in my stare.

"Ghost Girl doesn't want to be Ghost Girl," Eli guesses. "Normal ain't all it's cracked up to be, Hilda." He grins at the nickname.

Hilda? Oh no, he did not just shorten Mathilda to that awful nickname. "Do you want me to black the other eye for you?"

"I'd like to see you try," he counters, his eyes glowing with fury.

I take a step forward, but Caleb pulls me back. "Knock it off, Eli," he warns his brother. "I'll start calling you Elijah again if you don't."

"You always this hostile?" Eli asks me.

"Yeah, I am." I glare at him. "Deal with it."

"Why don't we go downstairs and eat?" Doc interrupts before Eli and I come to blows again. "Mattie, you must be starving."

Right on cue, my stomach growls. Mention food, and the bottomless pit opens its ugly mouth. I'm always slightly embarrassed by my stomach's need to be so vocal.

Mr. Malone laughs when Benny's belly starts complaining, too. "Let's go, guys. I picked up some Popeye's chicken before I came back."

I've seen the commercials on TV for Popeye's, of course, but my fried chicken experience has been limited to KFC. My mouth waters just thinking about the Colonel's fried chicken, causing my stomach to rumble loudly.

I follow Caleb down the stairs, with Eli right behind me. The hair on the back of my neck stands up, knowing he's watching me, and I get the distinct impression his eyes are well below my waist, which causes me to blush. I'm not at all comfortable with my reaction to this beautiful boy.

He is, in fact, too beautiful. It's those that you have to watch out for. I do distinctly remember my mama warning me about them from the time I was old enough to understand what she was saying. It's one of the few things I remember. Could be because I had several foster mothers say basically the same thing.

To try to distract myself, I look around at the house as we troop down the stairs. They are all hardwood and polished, the rail curved and stained in a darker color than the treads. The walls along the stairs and in the main foyer have wallpaper on them, but it's not cheap and gaudy like a lot of paper you see. It's elegant and fits the old-fashioned dark wood of the house.

The house doesn't look like it's in any kind of disrepair. Instead, the hardwood floors gleam, and the furniture is well taken care of. The house screams old money to me. I remember Doc saying something about it being one of the most haunted houses he'd ever come across. I guess I assumed it would be an old rundown house instead of the beautiful monument of a southern plantation it is. I have yet to explore the grounds, but I can't wait. I love architecture, and being here makes me feel like a kid on Christmas morning—aside from the ghosts, anyway.

Mr. Malone had laid out a feast on the dining room sidebar. My stomach growls appreciatively, but I'm almost afraid to sit down. The upholstery on the dining room chairs looks like the smallest stain would ruin the delicate material. The heavenly smells wafting up from the containers, however, make up my mind for me. I waste no time in grabbing a paper plate and a plastic fork before diving into the food. It feels like forever since I've eaten, even though I know I had dinner with Dan last night.

Once everyone is seated, Mr. Malone says grace, and I wait impatiently to dig in. The smell is divine. Once I see a chicken leg heading for Benny's mouth, I dive into my own food. A few minutes later, I look up to see everyone staring at me in amusement. I know I've been gobbling food faster than a NASCAR driver speeds down the track on race day, but still, it's rude to stare.

"Gosh, you eat more than me," Benny declares, eyes wide.

"I'm hungry," I defend. "I haven't eaten since last night."

"Mattie, you were out for three days, honey," Doc tells me.

"Three days?" I whisper.

Doc nods. "Yeah, you gave us all a scare. If you hadn't woken up soon, I was going to take you to the hospital."

"No more hospitals, thank you very much," I mutter. "I just had my last surgery, and I do not want to see the inside of one until I have to have my hands checked again."

"What happened to your hands?" Caleb asks curiously, staring at the bandages.

"Nothing." I sigh. I have no intention of going

into that. Doc's already blabbed enough about my personal life. They don't need all the gory details. "So, I assume you're the guys with the Angel blood Doc was telling me about?"

Caleb nods. "Yeah. You're not the only freak around."

I frown. I hate people referring to me as a freak, and I don't like Caleb referring to himself as one, either. He's not a freak.

"No, you're not a freak," I tell him. "Your brother, maybe, but not you."

"Hey!" Eli snorts. "I'm no more a freak than the Ghost Girl."

"Well, then, I guess you don't mind the lady whispering that you need to come visit her tonight, being used to it and all."

"W...what?" Eli glances all around him. "Where?"

I roll my eyes. There is no phantom lady, but he doesn't know that, and I grin. This might actually be fun.

"Yeah, I don't think you want to take her up on the offer," I tell him, working to keep my face straight. "She has a knife hidden behind her back."

Eli jumps up, looking everywhere. "Get away, you evil hag!"

"You are so punked." I laugh. "It's not even cold in here, the first sign of a ghostly presence. I thought you were an expert."

Caleb bursts out laughing, and Benny snorts milk through his nose when he giggles. Both Doc and Mr. Malone give up and laugh outright.

Eli glares at us all and stomps out of the room.

"I'm sorry," I say, wiping tears away. "I couldn't help it."

"He deserved it," Caleb wheezes, trying to stop laughing. "I don't think I've laughed this hard in forever. Thanks, Mattie."

"Okay, let's finish up here," Mr. Malone says between chuckles. "I'll put Eli's plate away, and he can eat later."

"I'll take it to him," I volunteer, regretting the words as soon as they leave my lips.

Mr. Malone raises his eyebrows.

"I think we got off on the wrong foot," I say. "The plate can be my olive branch."

Mr. Malone nods. "I appreciate that, Mattie. It's not often someone gets the best of my son, and he's reacting badly. He's not normally like that."

"I *am* normally like that." I laugh, especially when I see Doc nod vigorously. "You either love me or hate me, no middle ground to be had."

Mr. Malone gives me a look. "Amelia used to say that. You remind me of her."

"Who's Amelia?" I ask, remembering the earlier comment.

"She was my wife," he tells me. "She died a long time ago."

"I'm sorry," I say automatically.

"Thanks, but it was a long time ago. She was Caleb's mother. She and our baby died when they went off a cliff in an accident. We've moved on, and I found my Heather. She's Ben, Ava, and Eli's mother. She raised Caleb, and he thinks of her as his mom. Seeing you, though, reminds me of her so much."

I'm not sure what to say to that, so I pick up Eli's plate and go find him. Lord only knows what this conversation is going to be like. I need to learn to stop putting myself in situations where I can't control what happens.

But where would the fun in that be, the little devil on my shoulder whispers as I walk out of the room.

Chapter Eleven

Eli is nowhere to be found on the first floor, so I head outside. If I were pissed, it's where I'd go. I open the front door and step out. My mouth drops open. Oh, this can't be good.

I am not standing on the front porch of the plantation—instead I'm stumbling through the forest, running for my life. I know this even as I try to figure out what's going on. My side is in agony, and I see blood on my fingers when I pull my hand away. I recognize the wound. I've been stabbed. Again. What is it with me and knives?

It's cold, and I'm barefoot. Rocks and twigs stab at my sore feet as I run, and I try to make out the path I'm on. There's only a small sliver of moonlight streaming through the canvas of trees above me. I hear footsteps behind me and run faster, knowing with utmost certainty that if he catches me, I will die.

My heartbeat pounds in my ears, and I can hardly catch my breath as I stumble over more roots. He's whistling behind me, knowing I can't run much longer, not with the amount of blood I've lost. Anger burns through me, followed by despair. How can he do this? I loved him, and he's going to kill me. Tears sting my eyes, and I brush them away, hating the weakness that washes through me.

My dress catches on something and causes me to fall. I try to get up, but he's there in an instant. He pulls me up and into him. His arms circle around my waist, and for the barest moment I have hope, hope that he has given up on this madness, that he remembers he loves me, but that hope is dashed when I feel the knife press against me.

"Shh," he whispers. "It will be over soon. I promise it will not hurt for long, my love, and I will be here with you."

"Why?" My tears stream unbidden now. I am lost, unable to run anymore and weak from blood loss. "I love you. Why are you doing this?"

"What must be, will be," he tells me.

"I cannot understand this!"

"You do not remember, Lucy, but I do." His voice is a caress that strokes my skin, and I shiver even now, knowing he means to kill me.

"What?" I beg. "What is it I do not I remember?"

"You and I have danced this dance many, many times before," he says, the knife pressing deeper into my skin. "We have fought since the beginning of life, and it is our destiny to die, to atone for what we did."

"What did we do?" I ask softly. He is mad. Truly mad.

"We disobeyed, and now we must be punished."

"How is killing me a punishment for you?" I cry,

angry.

"Because I have loved you since the beginning of time." He presses a kiss against my temple. "I must always lose the one thing that is most important to me by my own hands. I am sorry, Lucy, but I must do this."

"Wait, please…"

He brings the knife up and plunges it into my chest. Pain explodes, and I cry out. He holds me close, and together we sink to the ground. I am cradled close to his chest, and he rocks me as the life seeps out of me. I look up into his beautiful face, the face I have held most dear since I was seven years old. The face of my friend, my husband, my murderer.

His aqua eyes burn with madness, and I am lost in them still. They are tortured and haunted. I long to cup his cheek and tell him everything will be all right, but I cannot do that this time.

"Cold," I mumble. "So cold."

"Shh, sweetheart," he soothes. "It is almost done. Just close your eyes and sleep, my love. Just sleep. All is well."

An arm grabs me and shakes me. Scared and confused, I turn and look straight into a pair of aqua eyes. I don't blink, but hit him as hard as I can. When he crashes to the ground, I start, coming awake. I see Eli sprawled on the ground, his nose bloody and fire spitting from his eyes.

"I'm so sorry!"

"What the hell?" he demands.

My hands are shaking, and it's all I can do not to run. His eyes look like those of the man who'd just stabbed me. My hand clutches my side. It still hurts, even though there is no wound there. My chest burns with pain as well. I stumble and fall backward, Eli's plate crashing to the floor of the porch. My breath comes out in short gasps. It hurts to breathe.

Eli approaches me as you would a wild animal, slowly and with a great deal of caution. "What happened?"

"I…I don't know," I answer honestly. "I came out to find you, but I wasn't here, I was somewhere else. I was *someone* else."

"Explain."

I shake my head, trying to clear it. "I was running through the trees, running from my…my husband. He wanted me dead."

"Mattie, you're not making sense."

"Don't you think I know that?" I glare, still clutching my side. "All I know is that it was as real as you are when he killed me."

"You had a vision?" the doc exclaims from the doorway. "Tell me."

I go into as much detail as I can, leaving out only that the man had aqua eyes the color of Eli's. I'm not sure why I don't tell Doc about that, but it isn't something I want to share.

"Maybe taking away one of your senses enhanced another one," Doc says softly. "By quelling the voices, we may have opened another way for them to communicate to you. You felt this woman die, like it was you?"

I nod, groaning on the inside. I go from having them hammering away at my skull to actually making me live out how they died? Just freaking awesome!

"Doc, I don't remember reading about any deaths like that in this house," Eli says thoughtfully.

"No, neither do I," he agrees, "but you remember me telling you how different Mattie is?"

He nods.

"She's like a beacon to spirits. There's an invisible light around her that calls to them. Her essence—her soul, if you will—is made up of ghost energy. They flock to her like bees to honey. I'm not surprised she's experiencing things outside this house."

Eli stares at me with an almost grudging respect. Bully for me.

"Mattie, why don't you go get some sleep?" the doc suggests. "It's late, and you need to rest after everything you've been through."

I am tired, more tired than I've ever been in my life, but I still need to talk to Eli to apologize for not hitting him once, but twice already.

"I will in a few minutes," I assure Doc, "but I need to talk to Eli first."

"You gonna hit me again?" he asks warily.

"No, not if you don't deserve it."

"I didn't deserve it the first two times!"

The doc snorts and turns around, going back inside and closing the door. Brownie points to Doc for knowing when to leave.

"I know that," I tell him softly. "That's why I came looking for you. I wanted to apologize for the beatdown you got."

"You barely scratched me," he denies.

"Whatever." I ignore the bloody nose he has at the moment from my last punch. "I just wanted to say I'm sorry. I know you didn't deserve it, but you startled me, and where I grew up, you learn to hit first before you get hit."

"Doc said you grew up in the foster care system," Eli says.

I nod and take a seat on the old-fashioned porch swing. "Yeah, it wasn't a pleasant childhood."

"My friend was in foster care." Eli sits down beside me, and that strange feeling starts to stir in my stomach. I get a little nauseated, and it concerns me. "He said it wasn't bad, though. He got placed with nice folks."

"There are some really good ones," I agree, "but for the most part, I ended up in ones where the parents only cared about the money the kids brought in every month. Some of them weren't bad, they at least left us alone and fed us, but some of them…" My mind shudders from the memories. "Let's just say we didn't walk away from those without scars."

I self-consciously rub my hands. This was a scar I'd live with forever. I'd been fooled into thinking Mrs. Olson cared about us and not the check. Little did I know she was a freak with split personalities who killed kids.

"I'm sorry."

"I don't want your pity," I say. "I wanted to apologize. It's not something I'd normally do."

"I can tell." He laughs. "You sound like you're choking when you say the word."

He's right about that. I hate apologizing.

Eli shifts on the swing, and I become even more

aware of him. It's like all the nerve endings in my body are firing to life, and I want to move closer, but at the same time, every warning bell I have is going off, screaming at me to run. It's the weirdest sensation ever.

"So, you guys can only see a ghost if it's evil?" I ask to distract myself from my body's reaction to him.

"Not evil, only the ones that have gone all vengeful spirit," he clarifies. "There are two types. When someone dies violently, they typically hang around, wanting revenge. Then you have the ones that are confused, and the longer they stay on this plane, the more confused, sad, and angry they become. When they reach the point where anger is all they feel, they start to hurt people to make them hurt like they do. When they start hurting people, that's when we get involved."

My thoughts immediately turn to Eric. "Does every ghost who doesn't cross over become a vengeful spirit?"

"Yeah, eventually, they all do. They can't help it."

"Is there any way to stop a ghost from becoming vengeful?"

"Why?" he asks, his eyes intent as they stare at me.

"I have a friend who's a ghost," I tell him. How can I protect Eric from himself? I've seen what he can do when he is spooked out. Thinking about it still terrifies me slightly.

"What?" Eli yells. "Mattie, you have to stop talking to her. She could kill you when she goes off the deep end."

"Eric would never hurt me," I tell him. "He saved my life."

"He will hurt you eventually," Eli says. "He won't be able to stop himself. When that happens, we'll have to track him down and take care of him."

"You hurt one hair on his head, and I'll beat you bloody!" There's no way Eli will ever get near Eric.

"You could try."

"I think I've already done more than try." I give him glare for glare.

"You're a vicious little thing, aren't you?" He shifts closer.

"Yeah, I am," I say, shifting closer myself.

We're almost nose to nose when we both still, feeling the massive temperature drop that swoops down upon us. A knife appears in his hand, and he stands up warily, looking around.

My eyes are locked on the other end of the porch. That same...thing that had been in my room and outside the restaurant is staring at me. Its body jerks and brings it closer. My breath hitches a notch. That thing touched me before, and I almost died. It isn't getting near me again.

"Eli," I whisper.

"I see it," he says grimly, his grip on the knife tightening. "Let's get inside, Mattie."

"It's not going to let us inside." I can feel the malice coming from it.

"Dad!" Eli yells at the top of his lungs. "Demon!"

It screeches, and three jerks later, it barrels down on us. Eli slashes at it with his knife. The blade slices through it, making it appear to shatter. It disappears, and I sigh in relief, but then I feel its putrid breath on my neck. I scream Eli's name, realizing it didn't die like I assumed.

It laughs, the sound a sickening rasp before it grabs me.

Chapter Twelve

The smell of rotten eggs fills my nose. I try to drag air into my lungs, but I can't. Laughter rings in my ears and rage pours into me. It's not my rage, but this thing's. It enjoys my pain, my desperation.

My knees buckle, and we go down. Its arms wrap tighter around me, and the noose around my neck tightens. Black spots start to appear around the edge of my vision. Eli is shouting, but I can't hear him around the buzzing in my ears. It is the voices of all the ghosts wailing in fear.

Focus, I tell myself, trying to stem the sheer terror overwhelming me. I'm not going out like this. No way do I survive everything I've been through, only to die by the hands of this stinky demon.

"Mattie!"

Dan? I see him running up the steps, coming straight for me. No! I don't want him hurt. I struggle harder, and the black ooze creeps up my arms, around my throat, turning from a liquid to a solid. It feels like fingers strangling me. Dan is almost here, and I fight harder, my need to save him stronger than the need to save myself.

Something inside snaps, and the black spots around my vision disappear. My body grows calm, and the cold seeps in. It's like thousands of ghosts are descending and latching on. The cold goes bone deep, so deep it burns. On the very edge of my vision, I see a light begin to grow and thicken, feel something start to build up inside. It's like I'm gathering all the cold into me, and the more it grows, the calmer I become.

I hear a blast, like a gunshot, and then I'm falling forward, trying to catch myself, but Eli is there, catching me before my face hits the floor. He yanks me up and literally throws me to his brother. He's holding a shotgun and slowly turning in all directions.

"Behind you!" I shout, but he is already falling and twisting, bringing the gun up and firing. The shot hits the creature square in the chest, and it explodes, flying into a thousand tiny wisps of smoke. My eyes widen. That's the same thing it did in my bedroom.

"Are you okay?" Caleb asks, concerned, I guess, because I'm coughing. That's the second time that thing has nearly choked me. It won't get a third try.

"Dear God, Mattie!" Dan yanks me out of Caleb's arms and wraps me in one of those bear hugs of his. "Are you okay? Did it hurt you?"

For five seconds, I bask here in his arms, then I remember what he did to me, and I withdraw. He feels the change and pulls back, chagrin in his eyes and on his face.

"I'm fine." I step away, closer to Eli. As much as

it hurts, I need to put distance between us. Dan hurt me more than anyone has in a long time. I haven't felt like this since waking up alone in a hospital and realizing my mom tried to kill me.

I want to curl up and cry like a baby, and it's not even stemming from the fact that he and Meg are seeing each other. I figured that out on the plane. He lied, kept this from me, and I trusted him. Everyone in my life has lied to me, and I thought Dan would never be one of them. He's supposed to be my rock, my anchor, the one person I can trust. He promised me he'd always be there for me, and then he went behind my back and betrayed me. How could he?

Caleb growls, and before I know it, a wall of muscles is in front of me. He and Eli have moved as one to stand in front of me. Dang, Eli has a cute butt. That random thought pops into my head, causing me to frown. Now, where did that come from?

"What are you two doing?" I demand. You can smell the testosterone in the air. I swear…boys!

"You looked ready to cry," Caleb explains.

"This is the guy who had you bawling, isn't he?" Eli chimes in.

"I do not bawl!" I deny hotly. What had I said while I was out and delirious? "Do you want me to hit you again?"

"You hit him?" Dan takes a step closer. "He didn't do anything to you, did he?"

"No." I shove both boys out of the way and step in between them. "I woke up, and it was dark. I didn't know he was in the room, and…why am I explaining this?"

Both boys shrug.

"What are you doing here, Dan?" I ask.

His face becomes the mask he wears when he's on the job, and all the anger I have flies out the window. Something is very, very wrong. Dan never gives me that look, no matter how bratty I'm behaving. Is it my mom? Does he know something?

"Is it my mom?" I ask softly.

"God, I wish it was your mom," he mutters. His eyes become haunted, turning nearly black.

"Dan, what's wrong?" I break free from Caleb and wrap my arms around Dan. "What's going on? Tell me."

He takes a shaky breath. "The PI, he found out…"

"Spit it out," Eli barks, his voice hard. I chance a look at him, and he's staring at the way Dan's arms are locked around me like a lifeline, his face creased in anger.

"Later, Mattie, I'll tell you later." Dan hugs me tighter before digging into his pocket and pulling out a bracelet of some kind. "Here's your gris-gris. Looks like you need it."

I eyeball the thing with disgust. Don't you have to believe in those things for them to work? I see an identical one on Dan's arm, and I look up questioningly. He has one? Dan has issues with ghosts, but he'll wear a gris-gris?

"I saw that thing, Mattie. If this keeps it away, I'll wear it," he tells me, understanding my question without my having to ask it. "Arm out, Squirt."

Like an obedient puppy, I hold out my arm, and he ties it around my wrist. The oddest sensation creeps over me, and I shudder. I almost tear it off when Eli puts his hand over my arm. "Don't," he says. "It works. I know it feels creepy, but you'll get used to it." He holds his own arm up, and I see a gris-gris on his arm, and Caleb sports one too.

"You don't have to believe in them for them to work." Eli smiles. "That's the great thing about Voodoo, it works whether you want it to or not."

Good God, the boy has dimples! His aqua eyes aren't staring at me with malice, but humor, and my insides clench, and those odd feelings flood my stomach again. What is wrong with me?

"Didn't you kill it?" I ask, ignoring the slight hesitation in my voice. At least I didn't stutter. How embarrassing would that be?

Eli shakes his head. "No, we only chased it off. Is it the same one you saw before?"

I nod. "Yeah, only this time it seemed faster."

"It would," Mr. Malone says from the doorway. "It's the house. Demons feed off the evil in the house and become stronger, faster."

"Dan?" The doc finally makes an appearance. About time. "I didn't expect you until tomorrow."

"Your Voodoo lady got these done early," Dan explains. "You said it was vital she gets it ASAP, so I drove straight here from Bourbon Street." He looks down at me. "Why haven't you answered any of my emails, texts, or voicemails? Do you have any idea how crazy I've been?"

I frown. "What are you talking about?"

"Mattie, I know you're pissed six ways to Sunday with me, but you promised you'd never do that to me again. Not after what happened."

"Dan, I don't have a phone, remember?"

"Uh, no, Mattie, you do. I overnighted it to Dr. Olivet. He was supposed to give you the phone and your new laptop."

"You see, Dan, about that..." Doc looks anywhere but at Dan. "Mattie wasn't in any condition to answer the phone."

It's Dan's turn to frown. "What happened?"

"Mattie has been unconscious for the last three days," he admits.

"*She what?*" Dan bellows, making me wince.

"It was the ghosts," Caleb tells him. "There were too many, and it overwhelmed her. It caused her to pass out into a kind of coma."

"And you didn't think to take her to the hospital?" Dan shouts.

"Chill, man, we fixed her up," Eli says. "Besides, she's fine. Woke up swinging and everything."

Dan eyes the busted lip and bloody nose Eli is wearing and gives him the best cop look he has. That look has made me squirm on occasion, but it doesn't faze Eli. He stares back, a challenge in his eyes.

"Before this comes to blows, let's go inside," Mr. Malone interrupts before either Dan or Eli can say anything else. "I'd like to ask a couple questions about that demon, since it seems to be following you, Mattie. We need to figure out how you picked it up."

"What do you mean, picked it up?" I ask, startled. Did it, like, latch onto me the same way ghosts do?

106

"There are lots of ways people can find a demon that decides they are a good meal to snack on, or even a host to hitch a ride with. We figure out how it found you, we might be able to get rid of it easier."

Eli groans. "Man, this was supposed to be a bag and tag, not a demon hunt."

"Bag and tag?" I ask.

"Find the vengeance ghost, which means bag it, and then kill it, or tag it," Caleb explains while giving his brother the stink eye. Caleb was the older of the two, in his early to mid-twenties, whereas Eli was about my age, give or take a year or so.

"Come on, Angel Boy," I say to Officer Dan. "You might learn something."

Leaving the boys behind to glare at each other, I follow Mr. Malone inside, hoping that at least *I* might get some answers.

Chapter Thirteen

We go back into the dining room, and I flop down in the first chair I come to. Eli and Caleb flank me on either side before Dan even has a chance to slide in next to me. These boys are serious, I realize. What in the world did I say while delirious? It must have been pretty bad if they're refusing to let Dan near me. Not that I planned on sitting next to him, anyway. I'm still beyond furious with him.

"Mattie, how many times now have you seen that thing?" Mr. Malone asks me.

"Three," I say and tell him about the previous two, going into as much detail as I remember, Dan throwing things in I hadn't been aware of, considering I almost died.

"Wait, wait, wait." Eli raises a hand to interrupt me. "You've only seen this thing when he's around?" He jerked his hand in Dan's direction.

I frown. "It attacked me on the porch, and Dan wasn't here."

"Yeah, he was," Caleb tells me. "He had just

pulled into the drive. I remember standing up to see who was here when I heard Eli shouting about demons."

Dan crosses his arms over his chest and glares at us all. I can sympathize; he's had a rough time of it lately dealing with the supernatural. This has to be so hard for him to sit and talk about. He refused to believe in anything supernatural until he met me. Sometimes, I still wonder if he doesn't try to logically explain my weirdness.

"Do you know what kind of demon it is?" I ask Mr. Malone to distract everyone. As mad as I am at Dan, I know what it feels like to be stared at and speculated about. It's not pleasant.

"It sounds like a protection demon."

Did he really say *protection* demon? "Uh, Mr. Malone, isn't that kind of the exact opposite of the whole evil demonic creature thing?"

He laughs. "I know it's hard to wrap your head around, Mattie. There are many different types of demons, all encircling the seven circles of hell. What you're describing is a third circle demon. It is called up by a summoner to protect someone from something or someone. The person it tries to kill is the thing or person it's protecting someone else against."

"So, someone thinks Dan needs protecting from *me*?" I ask, both startled and outraged.

"You got a hell of right hook, Hilda," Eli pipes up.

I'm up and twisting, but Caleb catches my fist before it connects with his brother's face. "Leave off, Elijah. Do you want to get another beatdown by a girl?"

"I didn't get a beatdown to begin with!" he denies hotly.

"So, you don't have a busted lip and black eye?" Dan scoffs.

Eli glares at him. "Nobody asked you."

"Can we get back to the discussion at hand?" Mr. Malone asks wearily, his face pained. Same look I get from Nancy sometimes.

"Dan, is there anyone you know who doesn't want Mattie in your life?" Doc asks.

Dan frowns, and then his face goes cold and bored—his cop look, I call it. Ohhh, Officer Dan does know something, and he's not gonna share. Don't think so.

"'Fess up, Officer Dan," I tell him. "What don't you want to say?"

"I don't know anyone who wants to hurt Mattie," he says, the bored tone matching the expression he wears on his face.

"That's not what he asked." Eli leans back in his seat, getting comfortable. "He asked if there's anyone who doesn't want her around you. Like maybe your new girlfriend?"

Points to Dan for not breaking the cop face. If you didn't know him, you wouldn't have noticed the slight tightening around his eyes to signal he's mad. Instead of giving Eli the reaction he's hoping for, Dan mimics the relaxed pose Eli adopted and shakes his head. "Meg and Mattie are friends. She'd never do anything to hurt her."

"You didn't really just say that?" I ask. Not hurt me?

"Mattie, she didn't intentionally…"

"Don't," I say softly. "If I never hear her name again, it will be too soon."

Dan gives me the same look Mr. Malone had given us all earlier, and I am so not in the mood for it. "Look, *Officer Dan*, if you can't deal with it, then you can leave right now. I'd be safer without you around, anyway."

He flinches but doesn't move. "Mattie, I told you once before, no matter how hard you push me away, I'm not going anywhere. I'm in it for the long haul."

"Yeah, you got that down pat, don't you?" Eli sneered. "Going out with her best friend is really in it for the long haul."

Dan shoots me an unbelievable look. He knows I don't go around telling complete strangers stuff. I can understand his disbelief.

"I was unconscious," I say. "They said I talked in my sleep."

"Yeah, you do," Dan agrees.

My eyes go a little round. Dan had spent many, many nights camped out at the hospital with me. What did I say? Then another reality hits me. If I talked in my sleep, he knew how conflicted I was about him, and he still started dating Meg. I blinked, my eyes burning with that realization. I would not cry, not here, not in front of these people.

"Want me to toss him out?" Caleb asks, seeing the hurt and confusion I'm trying so hard to hide.

I shake my head. "No, we need to figure this out." The sooner we do, the sooner I can send Dan on his way.

"Squirt…"

"No," I say. "I'm not talking about that right now. You need to 'fess up and tell us what you're trying to hide. You know something."

"Can I talk to you alone?" he asks.

"No," Eli and Caleb both say. I send them a glare. Something is going on with Dan, and he's not going to say anything around anyone. In some ways, he's as private as I am.

"Mattie, what if the demon comes back while you're alone with him?" Mr. Malone says. "We need to keep you where we can see you."

"It'll be fine." I stand up. "We'll go into the next room. If it comes back, one of us will scream our heads off."

No one in the room, except for Dan, looks happy with my decision, but tough. It's my life that's on the line, so if it means talking to Dan alone, I will. If he knows who's sending this thing after me, I need to know.

We go down the hall into what I guess would be called a parlor, maybe. The walls are covered with wallpaper. The floral pattern looks a bit tacky to me, but I've never liked anything with tons of flowers on it. The furniture is all dark mahogany that contrasts beautifully with the lighter wainscoting. It looks like something right out of a romance novel during the Civil War. Historical romances are a vice of mine, one I don't share with anyone.

"Mattie, we need to talk about this," Dan says, interrupting my silent musings. Leave it to the police officer to get right down to the heart of it. Problem is, I'm not ready to talk about it yet.

"No, I don't want to talk about that," I say, going to stand by the window. It looks out over a beautiful rose garden in full bloom. It's breathtaking. "What did you find out from your PI friend?"

He sighs. I can tell he's aggravated by the sound of it. "No, Squirt, we have to talk. I can't take this distance. I need you to forgive me."

I rub my arms, cold. Amazing how cold I am, even in the humid New Orleans temperatures. Doc says it's because of my soul being made up of ghost energy. Add that to the fact the little buggers flock to me like a kid to Disney World—I don't think I'll ever be able to get warm.

"Mattie!"

I turn to face him, leaning against the window frame. He doesn't look aggravated. He looks haunted. "Trust me, Dan, you really don't want to talk about this right now. You won't like what you hear."

"Please, I need you. Don't shut me out."

I laugh bitterly. "Then why would you do that to me, Dan? Why would you lie to me when you know how important honesty is to me?"

"I never lied to you."

"Hiding the truth from me is lying by omission," I say. "By doing that, you made a conscious choice to lie."

"We didn't think you could handle it…"

Another harsh laugh escapes. "You knew it was wrong, or you wouldn't have tried to rationalize lying to me. Why not just come clean and tell me you wanted to date my best friend?"

He sighs and runs a hand through his hair. It's

longer than he normally keeps it. "You had just gone through the worst nightmare of your life, and you were fragile. You might not want to admit that, but you were. Meg knew about your confused feelings when it came to me, and we both tried so hard to fight it, but we couldn't. It's so easy with Meg. We talk for hours and never run out of stuff to say. It's as natural as breathing with her."

"It's not easy with me?" I whisper, hurt flaring. I know I'm a mess, have trust issues like no one else, and I'm difficult on the best of days. No one but Dan has ever really cared enough to fight through those, or so I'd thought. I grew up knowing no one wanted me. That does terrible things to a person, things most normal people would never understand.

To live with the knowledge that you're a throwaway is awful. That's what I feel like, anyway. All my life I have moved from foster home to foster home, some good, most bad. Whenever I got too difficult to deal with, my foster parents would simply ship me back to be sent out to another temporary home. No one ever tried to get past my baggage, to care enough to try to love me.

Then I met Dan. No matter how hard I pushed, he stayed. I thought I'd finally found someone who cared, who wouldn't toss me back out onto the streets because it was too hard, but now he tells me how easy it is with Meg? I know I'm hard, I know this. I can't help it, but to hear him say it…it hurts. I love him more than I've ever loved anyone, and he doesn't want me because it's too hard?

"Mattie…"

"No," I cut him off, not wanting to hear anything

else. "I can't, not right now. This hurts too much."

"This isn't only about you, Mattie," he says softly. "It's about me too. You're not the only one who gets to be hurt and act like an ass."

My eyes narrow. I know I'm selfish, but I am not acting like that. I would never treat him the way he treated me. "Just go away, Dan."

He walks over and tries to pull me to him, but I refuse, stubbornly standing in my spot. I can't handle all that sympathy from the boy who has pulverized my heart.

"I never meant to hurt you, Mattie."

"You did, though," I say woodenly.

"I'm sorry."

And I know he is, and that's why this is so hard. He's truly sorry. I can see it shining out of those liquid brown eyes.

"Please, Mattie, I can't lose you."

I didn't want to lose him either, but I didn't see how we could go on from here. He'd broken me a little, and I needed to heal. I couldn't have him around if I had a shot of that.

"I want you to leave, Dan," I force the words out. "Leave me alone, please."

"Squirt…"

"No, Dan, I mean it. I want you to leave."

"No. I need you to forgive me, to talk to me."

"I can't forgive you, at least not yet. Maybe one day, but not right now. It hurts too much."

"Shh, Squirt, don't cry, please." He yanks me to him, and I bury my face in his shirt, soaking it. I missed him so much.

"I can't help it," I whisper. "You were the one

person I thought would never throw me away. I believed you when you said you were in it for the long haul. You made me believe you, Dan. No one's ever gotten past my defenses, but I let you in, and you broke me."

"God, Mattie, shh," he soothes. "I'm not throwing you away, can't you see that? I fell in love with someone. I couldn't help that. You and I, we're all messed up…"

I push him away and go back to staring out the window. He's right about us being messed up. We are, but hearing him say it makes the pain even worse. I'm a screwed up mess that no one can ever love, not really. Why did I ever let myself hope I could find a little happiness? Pointless.

"What did you find out from your PI?" I ask, changing the subject. I won't talk about this anymore. "Why did he want you to come down?"

Dan stands there for the longest time. I have no idea what's going through his mind, but I can't care about that right now. I have to have a little self-preservation. He's caused me too much pain as it is.

"He wanted to show me something," he says at last. "While he was looking through your mom's past, he found something out about my mom."

"Your mom or your birth mom?" I ask. Dan had never really wanted to look for his real parents, content in the fact his adopted family loved him as much as any biological parents could.

"Both," he whispers, almost too softly for me to hear. The agony in his voice has me turning to face him. That haunted look has come back into eyes. He looks like a little boy whose puppy had just died in front of him.

"Dan?"

"My mother didn't give me up for adoption," he tells me. "She died."

"That's a good thing, isn't it?" I ask. At least he wasn't abandoned.

He shakes his head and takes a step, but he stumbles a little. I reach out and grab him, leading him over to the settee. It's not often something knocks Officer Dan off his game.

"Mom told me when I was little that she'd gone through hell and back to find me. I always assumed she meant my biological mother had issues giving me away. I never thought..." he trailed off before taking a deep breath. "Phil knows some pretty seedy people, and in trying to track your mother, my mother's name came up. He...he found out a lot of stuff."

I had a feeling this was so not gonna be good.

"We never knew Mom had a sister until she died. I was about nine years old, so I remember the day she got a phone call and burst into tears. She cried for weeks. Dad knew she had a sister, but they'd never met. Mom said all the pictures of the two of them were destroyed in a fire, and since they'd grown up, they didn't really spend any time together. They'd had a falling out, and she hadn't spoken to her sister in years."

This is hard for him. He's practically forcing each word out of his mouth. I can feel his pain just as I feel the pain from the ghosts I do my best to ignore. He's hurting right now, and he's hurting a lot. My first instinct is to hold him, to try to help him, but I resist. I let my own self-preservation instincts kick in. I can't let him in any more than he already is.

"Phil discovered a check my mom had written to a Claire Hathaway." Dan looks me straight in the eye as he drops his little bomb.

"What?" I whisper. His mom knew mine? Had given her money...my eyes widen. No, it can't be...no.

"Claire Hathaway, born Amanda Sterling, was my mother's sister." Dan jumps up and walks over to the window. "She helped your mom take you, gave her the money to start over."

That's why his mom freaked that first day she met me and why she's gone out of her way since then to avoid anything to do with me. She knew who I was. Did she blame me for her sister's death?

"I don't know what to say," I murmur.

"It gets worse." His voice is flat, dull. He turns away, staring at nothing.

Worse? How much worse can it get?

"Phil started to look into my mom's past to try to figure out where they took you from. He found out my mom...she...she..."

"Dan?" What is so awful he can't say it?

"She murdered my birth mother," he whispers brokenly. "My mom, who has taken care of me since I was born, murdered my birth mother and stole me."

Oh, God, it did get worse. I don't even have words. Instead I wrap my arms around him, nestling my face into the warmth of his back. It's the only thing I know to do.

118

"She killed her, Mattie. Held her hostage until I was born, then killed her and put her in a car and forced it off the cliff. The car caught fire, and the damage was so bad, the police only found shards of bone. They didn't even blink when there wasn't a baby. The fire burned so hot, they assumed any traces had burned to ashes."

"I'm so sorry," I tell him. "I...what are you going to do?"

"I don't know, Mattie...she's my mom..." He shakes his head. "I know what I *should* do, but she's *my mom.*"

"Are you sure about this?" I ask. "Maybe he made a mistake..."

"No, Mattie, he didn't make a mistake. Phil talked to people who helped her."

"But why?" I ask. "Why would she do that?"

"I don't know. What do I do, Mattie?"

I have no idea. "Did Phil tell you anything about your birth mother?" I need to distract him from thinking about his mom. It's tearing him up inside. Later, I'll let myself react to the fact his mom helped steal me from my real family, but right now, he needs me. Even if I can't forgive him, he needs me, and I won't turn away from that. Not now.

"Yeah, he told me her name. It was Amelia Malone."

"The hell you say!"

We both turn to see Caleb and Eli staring at us, shocked, angry, and confused.

Oh, Lord, this is not going to be good.

Chapter Fourteen

Looking from Dan to Caleb, it is so obvious they're brothers. I'd been comparing them all day, convincing myself I had been seeing Dan only because I missed him so much. There is no denying the truth, though. Dan has just found his family.

Not that everyone appears happy about that fact. Dan has his arms crossed, his cop face firmly in place. Eli looks like he wants to hit someone, and Caleb only stares. I'm not sure what Caleb is thinking. He has a pretty decent cop face himself.

Mr. Malone has a completely different reaction when Caleb tells him about Dan's revelation. He can't seem to stop staring at Dan. I can tell he wants to hug him, but he's restraining himself. Dan isn't exactly being very talkative, either. He's refusing to answer questions, and I know why. He doesn't want anything to happen to his mom. Dan shut down once Eli said they needed to call the police and start an investigation.

It has to be very hard for Mr. Malone. He's just been informed his wife was murdered, his son stolen. The need for justice, for revenge, has to be burning inside, but he is restraining himself. They're discussing the woman who raised his son, loved him like her own, but Ann Richards is also the woman who took everything from him, from Caleb. I'm not sure how he's keeping it together, honestly.

Dan dropped a huge bombshell on me too, and I'm not handling it at all well. Mrs. Richards helped her sister take me from my parents. Who's to say she didn't kill them too? I hadn't been able to ask Dan anything else about it once Eli bellowed and brought his dad running, but that question has been running around and around in my head. Does Dan know who my parents are? I want to be selfish and demand answers, but I'm doing my best to be as un-Mattie-ish as I can. He needs to talk to the Malones.

When Mr. Malone begins to talk, I slip out of the room. They need to be alone. I go hunting for Doc. He said something about going to the control room. I figure it has to be on the main floor. Problem is, the main floor is freaking huge. I wander down a hall and find myself in a library. The shelves go from floor to ceiling with books older than any I've ever seen. The pages are yellowed on one whole section. The furniture is dark cherry wood and there are two oversized stuffed chairs in front of a massive fireplace. I could live in this room.

I trail my fingers across the books as I walk the length of the room. They feel so soft, so old. This is what I always imagined a library should look like. It's what I plan on having someday. I love books and have recently started writing. No one knows how much I love books, not even Dan. Bookworms aren't "cool," so I pretend I hate them. Since I can't draw, I've been writing things down. It's slow, as it's still hard to hold a pen or pencil for any length of time, but it helps me get some of my anger out and to keep my fingers from stiffening up. Who knows, maybe I'll write the next *Twilight* or something.

"How are you holding up, kiddo?"

Whirling, I see Doc standing a few feet away. I hadn't heard him walk up behind me.

"You scared me," I say and turn back to staring at the books. I really don't want to talk about my feelings with anyone. Well, I would with Dan if I was still on good speaking terms with him, but since I'm not, I'm stuck with only me.

"I know Dan is center stage right now, but you got handed some pretty heavy news too," Doc continues, ignoring my hint that I don't want to talk. "To find out your mother isn't really your—"

"I already knew that," I interrupt him.

"How?"

"She told me," I whisper. In all the years I've had this gift, my mom's ghost had never visited me until that night in the hospital after the kidnapping. "That's why Dan was looking into my past. He was trying to find my parents."

"Do you want to talk, Mattie?" he asks.

"This is a bunch of BS!" Eli storms into the room and hurls himself onto one of the couches.

I sigh. I should have known my little hideaway wouldn't last.

"You don't think Dan is your brother?" Doc

asks.

"He looks just like Caleb," Eli spits out. "What's BS is the fact that he won't even talk about calling the cops."

"It's his mom," I tell Eli. "Of course he doesn't want to call the cops."

"She's not his mom! She freaking killed his mother!"

I sigh. Eli is so angry, he's not thinking it through. "Yeah, I get that, and so does Dan, but she is his *mother*," I stress the word. "She raised him, and he loves her. Despite everything, to him, she is his mother."

"She—"

"Shut up!" I interrupt. "What if we were talking about your mom? What if you found out today the woman you call mom murdered your birth mother? You've spent the last seventeen years in her care. She's loved you, been there for you, and to you, she's your mom. Would you want to turn her in? Think about that before you judge Dan or anybody else."

"Why are you defending him?" Eli demands. "After what he did to you—"

"He's still my family," I say. "No matter what Dan does or doesn't do, he's family. I may never forgive him for what he did, but he's family."

"I thought you'd already forgiven him." Eli frowns at me.

"No," I whisper. He thinks being with me is hard. Dan just keeps hurting me whether he realizes it or not. I'm done being hurt.

"What the hell did he say to you in there before

Caleb and I got there?" Eli's eyes are narrowed on my face. My expression must have given something away.

"Doesn't matter," I tell him. "Dan and I are done. I'm not sure we can even be friends anymore."

"Mattie…"

I look up into Dan's big old puppy dog eyes, burning with pain. I want to take the words back, but I can't. I won't. Caleb and Mr. Malone are standing behind him in the hallway, and I turn away, unable to bear the look in Dan's eyes. "So, Doc, tell me about the house. I came here to help you, so tell me what I'm looking for."

Doc heaves a sigh. I think he really wanted to talk about my feelings. *So not going there, Doc.*

"Let's all have a seat," Doc says. "We might as well be comfortable, as none of you have heard this story, and it will take a while to tell."

I walk and sit on the opposite side of the couch from Eli. Dan heads for the open spot beside me, but Caleb gets there first, which earns him a glare from Dan. I really, really want to know exactly what I said while I was out.

Once everyone is seated, Doc goes to stand by the fireplace. I think he does it unintentionally, but he always seems to find the one place to sit or stand that makes him mesmerizing, impossible to take your eyes away from him. And when he starts to speak, you're hooked like a crack mule.

"I was sitting at home in front of my fireplace about a month ago, going over some old texts I had recently acquired from an estate sale in Dublin, when my phone rang. It was a rather bizarre call. An old friend of mine I hadn't heard from in a while was babbling on the other end about evil. It took me almost an hour to calm Stew down enough to talk to him."

Dr. Olivet shifts and leans into the mantel. His face is soft, inviting, but it's his voice that's so hypnotic. We're all listening intently to his story.

"Stew and I are old college buddies. We don't talk as much as we used to since he and his wife moved to England. I only get to hear from him sporadically, which was why his call at midnight was so startling." He shakes his head and stares out the window. "He and his wife inherited a property back here in the States, and they decided to sell it. Stew had been laid off, and they needed the money. He came back state-side to get the estate ready for sale. It hadn't been occupied in over ten years, but there was a trust set up that makes sure repairs and maintenances were completed regularly."

"Hold up, Doc," Eli interrupts. "This house has a trust fund? Who does that?"

"Rich people," I tell him. "Now shut up and let Doc finish."

He glares are me, but shushes.

"The attorney who handled his cousin's will refused to meet him at the house and had Stew pick up the keys at his office. Stew thought it a little odd, but dismissed it. When he arrived at the house, night had fallen. The house was dark, and he told me he almost didn't go in. He got an ominous feeling, but shook it off. He said he'd been watching too many scary movies lately and attributed his unease to that."

Unease? This house is freaking creepy.

"Everything was fine for the first few days," Doc continues. "There was a lot to do in order to get the house ready for sale, and Stew kept busy. It was on his fourth night in the house that things started to get weird. Nothing too much, just little things. He heard creaking on the stairs and told himself it was the house settling. The next morning when he woke, the kitchen was a mess. The fridge was open, its contents scattered. Dishes lay broken on the floor, the chairs moved around. He assumed someone had broken in and reported it to the police. Things began to get a little hairier after that. Doors he'd closed would be open five minutes later, the faucets in the house constantly dripped even after they'd passed inspections from several plumbers. The temperature in the house fluctuated from cold to freezing even if he turned off the AC."

"Those are classic haunting signs." Caleb frowns. "Why didn't he call you earlier?"

"Stew didn't believe in ghosts," Doc says simply, "and it almost got him killed."

I look over at Dan, who is as engrossed in the Doc's spiel as the rest of us. Sometimes I wonder what he thinks now that he knows the spookier side of life is real. Does he regret meeting me because I tore away his fundamental beliefs, especially since he started seeing demons himself? I don't know.

"Stew being Stew, ignored the obvious," Doc continues, interrupting my thoughts. "He decided it was only his own imagination running wild. He continued working on airing out the rooms and managing the construction crews that were modernizing some of the rooms to make the house more marketable. A week into the construction, his crew quit. When asked, they refused to go back into the house. They said it was haunted. Several of the workers swore they saw things, felt things, and one said he'd been pushed down the stairs by an unseen force. It all sounds very generic, like something you'd see in a B movie, and that is what Stew attributed it to. There were stories about the house, and the workers had been hesitant to go into the house from the beginning. He decided they'd let their imaginations get the best of them.

"He went to bed that night thinking people were too superstitious. A short while later, the cold woke him up. His teeth were chattering, and when he turned on the lights, he saw frost all over the windows and the mirror. The bathroom water was running, and he went to turn it off. As soon as he stepped over the threshold, something pushed him, hard. He went stumbling, and the lights went out. He fell and tried to get back up, but he felt someone kick him in the ribs. When he got up and turned the lights on, there was no one there, but he had a huge bruise forming where he'd felt the shoe connect with his ribs. He turned off the water and searched the house, thinking someone had gotten in, but found no one.

"The footsteps started as he was checking the locks on the first floor. He could hear them run from one end of the house to the other above him. He ran upstairs, but found no one. He checked each room, but again, they were empty. By this point, he started to get a little freaked out. He headed back to his own room. When he reached the middle of the hallway, every door on the second floor slammed open. Stew did what any sane person would do. He ran. Laughter followed him. He said he could feel hands grabbing at him, but saw no one. He made it halfway down the stairs when he was shoved, causing him to fall. This is where it got a little fuzzy for him. He'd hit his head, and his vision was blurry, but he said he saw someone standing on the stairs, smiling at him. It appeared to be a man, but his face was twisted. Stew said he hadn't known what evil felt like, but he learned that night as he stared up into the man's face.

"He dragged himself to the front door and then out of the house. It took him a bit to clear his head enough to drive, but he managed to get to a hotel and call me. I've never heard him so scared before. It really shook him up."

"I don't understand, Doc." Mr. Malone frowns. "It sounds very generic, like he really was just spooked and probably scared himself into thinking the place was haunted. He admits hitting his head. Isn't it possible he imagined the person standing above him?"

"It's possible," the doc agreed, "but you don't know Stew like I do. He is the most down-to-earth person I know, and he'll find an explanation for anything remotely supernatural rather than admit it's something paranormal."

"Doc, I hate to say it, but we've been in this house for a week and haven't encountered one single ghost." Caleb shakes his head. "Even our equipment is silent. I'm not sure there's anything here."

"Mattie?" Doc looks at me, and I sigh. He wants to know if I saw anything remotely like his friend had. I did, but I don't want to tell him. I want to get out of this house. I want to question Dan, and I want to talk to his mom. She knows who my parents are. If I tell Doc what I saw, he'll dig in and refuse to leave. But I can't lie to Doc. He's one of the few people left I trust.

"I saw a man standing on the front porch when we arrived. At least I think it was a man; it was hard to tell. He was full of hate. I could feel it even inside the truck. He enjoyed my pain, wanted me to come inside. If I hadn't passed out, I'd have demanded Caleb take me back to the airport and ran as far and as fast I could."

"No offense, Mattie, but I don't buy it," Eli tells me. "There's no activity in this house."

I tune out what Doc says. I can see a woman standing in the corner of the room. Her face is pale, the eyes bruised. She's wearing a very old dress, maybe late 1800s? I don't think anyone realizes how cold it is in here. They're too busy arguing about whether there are ghosts here. I'm still not quite sure how their gifts work, but if they can't see this, then maybe she's not a bad ghost? Just lost and in need of help.

Her eyes are full of pain. They look so haunted. I may not be able to hear her, but I can feel her overwhelming grief. Her lips are moving, but all I hear is a mumbled whisper. I frown. What is she saying? She keeps pointing at the wall behind me. I turn and look, but there are only paintings hanging there. What does she want?

"Mattie?" Doc interrupts me. "What are you looking at?"

I ignore him and turn back to the woman, only this time I see someone standing behind her. The malice coming from him is intense, and I shrink back against the couch cushion. It isn't the same man I saw on the porch, but he's dangerous. This is one who could and would hurt me or anyone in this room. His attention is focused on the woman, though, not us.

She doesn't see him. Why doesn't she see him or sense him or something? She's shouting at me, and I feel a stab of pain shoot through my temple. I raise my hand to grab it, remembering the night Eric put me in the hospital.

"Caleb, turn on your EVP sensor," Doc barks. I hear a shrill wail start, and I'm pretty sure it's the EVP sensor.

"What the...?" Caleb whispers.

"There's something here with us?" Doc asks me.

I nod. The man standing behind the woman turns and looks at me. He smiles and starts forward, his hand outstretched. I jump up and start to back away. Why can't they see him? Aren't they supposed to see evil ghosts? This is as evil a ghost as I've ever seen.

Caleb moves in front of me, and the red and green lights on his device go crazy. "What is it, Mattie, what do you see?"

"You don't see him?" I whisper. He's so close.

"No." Caleb frowns. "I can't see—"

There's a thump upstairs, and then the lights go out, plunging us into darkness.

Hands grab me and drag me from the room.

Chapter Fifteen

I groan and roll over onto my back. Did I hit my head? I open my eyes, but it's too dark to see anything. The air is musty and stale. My bandages have come unraveled somehow, so I can feel the loose dirt under my fingers. How did I get here? I was in the library and then...ohmygosh! I scramble up and bang my head against something. Pain explodes, and I fall back down. *Oww*.

My knees protest when I push myself up, and take a deep breath. I wrinkle my nose at the smell. It's not too bad, though. I've been in worse places. The thing that concerns me most at the moment is how and why I'm here. I was dragged out of the library by someone, but who? Or what? And are they down here too?

It's freezing, so I assume I'm not alone, but since Eli and Caleb tattooed me, I can't hear the ghosts like I did. It's frustrating and more than a little scary. As much as I hate what I can do, I rely on it to keep me safe, especially since I discovered they can cause me harm. Now I'm stuck with my ghost

Spidey senses at half-mast. Not at all good. Not in this house.

"Hello?" I whisper.

Nothing. I hear nothing. I stand up slowly and walk with my hands out in front of me until I hit the wall. I move along the wall, looking for either a light switch or a door. The sooner I can find my way out of here, the better. The walls themselves are made of dirt, so I'm thinking I might not be in a basement but a cellar. A lot of old houses have them in addition to a basement. Back in the 1800s they were used to store things that needed to be in a cool, dry place, like vegetables and sometimes even ice.

Wind catches my hair and blows it back. I stop and take a deep breath. It's not the wind. There's no wind down here. Plus, there's a stench. It's an awful smell that makes me choke a bit. Not nearly as bad as demon stink, but bad enough to make the contents of my stomach want to come back up. *Just keep moving, Mattie*, I tell myself. *Keep moving.* I start forward again, a little faster this time. Definitely not a nice ghost. I'm starting to pick up emotions, and they are full of rage.

Fingers reach out and tickle up my arm, causing me to shiver. The cold seeps through my skin and settles into my bones. I'm shaking from cold when I force my feet to start moving again. My eyes have adjusted to the darkness, and I can make out shapes. Not sure what they are, but I think I see steps a few feet in front of me.

More hands tug at me, twisting in my hair. Fear curls through me, but I refuse to panic. I need to get up the stairs and out of this place. It's a bad place, full of pain and rage.

Yes, I make it to the steps! I run up them as quickly as I can. It's definitely a cellar. The doors are right above me. I push, but I can't get them open. I hear chains rattle. I'm locked in? Oh no, no, no! I can't be locked in.

"Hey, can anyone hear me?" I shout while rattling the doors. Of course, they can't, since they're probably all inside searching the house looking for me and I'm out here. And I'm defenseless. Thanks to Eli and Caleb, I can't hear the ghosts anymore, which puts me at a distinct disadvantage. They are so gonna fix this when I get out of here.

"Somebody help me!" I scream out into the night. God, how long will it take them to figure out I'm not in the house? I shake the doors again, disgusted.

What am I—a shriek escapes as I go hurtling backward, fingers wrapped in my hair and pulling me down the steps and deeper into the darkness. My body makes contact with each step, as does my head. I'm on the floor being dragged by the hair. Panic takes over and I scream, loud and long, trying to fight the hands grabbing at me. There have to be dozens of them. I can smell the awful scent everywhere, feel the malice coming from the ghost hauling me along the floor deeper into the cellar.

Light floods the cellar, and I scream, fighting harder. I can see the thing dragging me, and I flinch. It's a man, his face covered in dirt and grime. He has a machete in one hand, and his other is firmly entangled in my hair. His eyes are hollow and mean. He grins down at me and raises the knife.

Something slices through him, and a brilliant white light emanates from it. I blink, and I'm free. Strong arms haul me up and pull me close. Oh, God. I thought no one was going to find me. Aqua eyes stare down at me, and all I can do is cry like a girl.

"I didn't think anyone was going to find me," I say between hiccups.

"I'll always find you." Eli smiles down at me. "Always."

I'm ripped from Eli's arms and enfolded in a bear hug. Dan. I can smell his cologne. It's very woodsy, just like him.

"Took you long enough," I mumble.

"I swear to God, I'm going to kill you!" Dan whispers. "Didn't I promise to do exactly that if you scared me this bad again?"

"I'm fine, Dan," I tell him. "Really."

"How did you get down here?" he demands, refusing my attempts to free myself. He's anchored me to him in a death grip.

"I don't know. I was upstairs one second and down here the next. Can we get out of here, please?"

"Sure, Squirt," he says and ushers me up the stairs. Eli follows, and I get the distinct impression his eyes are where they aren't supposed to be. I glance back, and sure enough, he's staring at my behind. I clear my throat, and he looks up sheepishly.

"You're shaking," Dan fusses, urging me along the path and back inside the house.

"Of course, she's shaking. She just got attacked." Eli rolls his eyes. "The thing was dragging her deeper into the cellar when *I* found her."

"I was right behind you," Dan snarls. "You just got two steps ahead of me."

"Does it really matter who found her?" Mr. Malone asks. "She's safe now, and that's all that counts."

Doc thrusts a cup of something very hot into my hands. "Chamomile tea," he says. "It'll help."

Dan pushes me down onto one of the couches. We're back in the library, I realize. He sits next to me this time. I'm trapped between him and the couch arm. Eli glares at him, but for once Dan ignores him. He's completely focused on me.

"Are you sure you're okay, Squirt?" he asks, the concern clear in his eyes.

I nod and take a sip of tea. "Yeah, I'm good. Eli sent the ghost running."

"No, I killed it," he corrects me. "I sliced it through with a blessed blade. Kills them dead."

"Thank you," I tell him.

"You're welcome, Hilda."

I close my eyes and count to ten. He has just saved my life. It's okay. I'm not that mad. Oh, why am I even bothering? I'm up before Dan can stop me, my fist barreling down at Eli. He grins, catches my hand, and twists, pulling me down on top of him.

"Uh-uh," he whispers. "You're not getting the drop on me again, Mattie."

I'm extremely aware of being pressed against him, the feel of him under my fingers, his breath against my cheek. My stomach clenches, and I get a little nauseated again. Why does this happen when I get close to him?

"Stop flirting with your brother's girlfriend before you get hurt, Eli," Mr. Malone tells him sternly.

"Dan's not my boyfriend," I say softly, staring into Eli's gorgeous eyes.

"You sure he knows that?" Caleb asks snidely.

I glance over at Dan and see him standing a few inches from us, his face enraged. He has no right to be mad at me. He was the one who made the decision to date someone else.

"Be careful of her hands," Dan growls, reaching down and yanking me up. "She's just had surgery. Where are your bandages?"

"Where's your gris-gris?" Doc asks, alarmed.

Dan had tied it on top of my bandages. It must have come off when the bandages did.

I shrug. I have no clue where either are.

Dan is gently running his hands over mine, checking for injuries. He pauses over the fresh scar on my wrist. Oddly, I don't shiver when Dan touches me, but when Eli does, it's all I can do to keep from a full body shudder. Dan's touch makes me feel safe and loved. Eli's is more edgy, dangerous, and a little scary because of the emotions it evokes. Dang it, I wish Meg and I were still on speaking terms. I need to talk to a girl about this stuff.

"I'll head out and get you some new bandages first thing in the morning," he says and leads me back over to the couch. "How did you lose your bandages and your gris-gris?"

"I guess somewhere between the house and the cellar," I say. "I don't remember getting there, though. It was like I blinked, and then I was in the dark."

He ran his thumb over my forehead. "You got a goose egg here. Did you hit your head too?"

My hand comes up to touch the sore spot, and I hear Caleb gasp. I quickly move my hands to my lap, trying to hide them. There are still several places that have pins in them and look a little deformed. I'm very self-conscious of them.

Dan shoots Caleb a glare. "Don't worry about it, Mattie. They look fine."

I nod, but refuse to meet anyone's eyes. Not something I'd planned on sharing with them. "Look, guys, can we pick this up in the morning? I'm tired, and I want to get some sleep."

"Of course," Doc murmurs. "I don't think you should be alone, though, Mattie. Something in this house seems to have targeted you, and we still haven't dealt with the demon that's hunting you."

"I'll be with her," Dan says. "She'll be fine."

"I don't think that's such a good idea." Mr. Malone frowns. "The demon shows up when you're around, Dan. You might not be the safest person for her right now. Caleb and Eli can watch over her."

"Over my dead body," Dan hisses. "I'm not trusting her safety to anyone but myself."

"Son," Mr. Malone steps forward, and Dan flinches back against the couch. Mr. Malone stops, looking sad. "Your brothers will protect her with their lives. I promise she'll be safe with them."

"No," Dan refuses stubbornly. "She's not going anywhere with anyone but me."

"What if Caleb and Eli take shifts with you?" Doc suggests. "That way, if the demon shows up, you'll have someone there to help you."

"It's a good plan, Dan," I tell him softly.

"Fine," he growls.

"I'll take the first shift," Caleb says before Eli can. I think Caleb knows Dan might do physical harm to Eli at this point.

I stare from Dan to Caleb to Eli. It's going to be a long night.

Chapter Sixteen

After changing into my favorite PJs, I walk back into my room to find Caleb and Dan staring at each other. I bet neither has said a word since I left them fifteen minutes ago. It's so sad. Just seeing them together, it's obvious they're brothers. Neither knows what to say to the other.

Awkwaaarrrd.

"Caleb, can Dan and I have a few minutes alone?" I ask.

Caleb frowns. "I don't know, Mattie."

"Please?" I give him my best pleading look.

He sighs, but gives in. "I'm going to be right outside the door. Don't upset her." He glares at Dan.

Dan's eyebrows shoot up, and he gives me a questioning look.

I shrug. "You know I talk in my sleep, but apparently I do it when I'm unconscious too. They won't tell me what I said about you."

"I can guess." Dan sinks down onto the bed. "I'm sorry, Mattie. I really screwed up, didn't I?"

"Dan, I don't want to talk about that right now," I say and crawl under the covers. "It's too painful. What about you? How are you? Do you know what you're gonna do?"

"They think I'm a monster," he whispers.

"No, they don't." Well, maybe the boys do, but not Mr. Malone. He's just grateful his son is alive.

"Maybe I am a monster." He sighs and lies back, tucking his hands under his head. "She's my mom. I know what she did is wrong, but she's my mom, Mattie."

"It's okay, Dan." I roll to face him. "I understand. You love her."

"It's not okay, Squirt." His voice is a little hoarse. "What she did to me, to the Malones, to you. None of it's okay."

Selfish Mattie has been quiet long enough. "Dan…did your PI…did he find out who my parents are?"

"No. He said he's hit dead ends. The one lead he has is my mom, and Phil said he'd leave it up to me to figure out where to go from here."

His mom knows who my parents are. I want to demand he take me to her this minute so I can get answers, but I can't do that. He's hurting so much right now. Even I'm not that selfish when it comes to the people I love. And I do love him.

"Caleb and Eli are really, really mad," he says. "Do you think they'll call the police? I've been debating if I should call Mom all night."

I don't think Caleb would without talking to his dad. He's too much like Dan. Eli, on the other hand…he'd do it. "Call her. Don't ask her any questions if you don't want to, but I think Eli is mad enough that he might call. He'd be trying to do the right thing, but I don't think he's thinking it through, thinking about all the pain he's going to cause you, your dad, and your brother."

"Oh, God—Dad," Dan whispers. "I haven't even thought about him."

Mr. Richards will be devastated. He loves his wife, his family. Nothing is more important to him. This is going to rip them to pieces.

Dan sits up and fishes his phone out of his pocket and stares at it. "I know I shouldn't warn her. I know that, but…"

"Doesn't matter what she did, Dan, she loves you. I know that better than anyone else in this house. I've seen her look at you. What she did was beyond wrong, but she's been a good mom. I know it's hard, I know you don't want to turn her in, I know all these things, but I know in the end you'll do the right thing because of who you are, who *she* raised you to be. Doesn't mean you can't warn her, though."

"Mattie, if she runs, we lose our only lead on your parents." He looks so serious, so sad. I can't believe he's thinking about me right now.

"Your PI is good. He'll find something," I say, knowing in my heart he won't. The truth of my parents will probably disappear with his mom.

He stares at me, his heart in his eyes. He's broken. This broke him. I want to curl myself around him and tell him it's going to be okay, but I force myself to stay still. "What…what do I say to her?" he whispers.

142

Like I know? Why do people always insist on asking me stupid questions like that?

"I don't know," I say at last. "Just call, and you'll know what to say." Pretty sure he won't, but it's the best I've got right now.

He sighs and finds the number in his address book. He puts the phone on speaker and then lays it down on the bed. I'm surprised he's using speakerphone. Dan's usually a very private person.

"Dan?" Mrs. Richards voice comes through.

"Hey, Mom."

"Honey, where are you? I talked to your captain today, and she said you'd requested a few weeks off to deal with a personal matter. What's wrong? How can I help?"

She sounds so worried and genuinely concerned. Dan closes his eyes, a tear finally slipping down his cheek.

"I'm in New Orleans, Mom."

"New Orleans?" Her voice has gone soft. "Why are you in New Orleans, Daniel?"

"I know about Amelia Malone."

"Who?"

Even I'm impressed with how confused she sounds. *Points to you for being a great liar, Mrs. R.,* I think snidely.

"Amelia Malone, Mom," he whispers hoarsely. "My birth mother, the woman you killed."

"I don't know what you're talking about…"

"Don't, Mama," he says harshly. "I already spoke with the people who helped you. I know Claire Hathaway is your sister and that she helped you."

"Did that...*girl*...put you up to this?" she demands, anger in her voice. "I knew the minute I laid eyes on her she was trouble. You should have listened to me about her."

She means me. I flinch at the accusation in her tone.

"I was helping Mattie try to find her father," he says. "The PI looking into it found out what you did to me *and* to her. We know you helped your sister take her from her family."

"You don't know anything about it!" his mother shouts through the phone. "Those people...we saved her, saved *you*."

"Saved me? You killed my mother and stole me from my family! Why, for God's sake, would you do that?"

"Daniel, I love you," she whispers. "You are my son, and nothing is going to change that. What I did, I did out of love and desperation. You don't know what kind of people they were, what they did..." She sighs. "I gave you a good life, loved you. Doesn't that count for something?"

He hangs his head. He's so heartbroken. I sigh and give up. Crawling behind him, I wrap my arms around him, fitting my legs against his own. My head rests on his back.

"Mama, I love you. That's why this is so hard."

"Are you...are you going to turn me in, Dan?" Her voice is small, hesitant.

"I'm a police officer. I know I should, but—"

"But nothing," she says hurriedly. "You're my son, and I'm your mother. Nothing can be done about the past. What's done is done, Dan. We're a family. Me, you, your father, and your brother. We're happy. Isn't that enough?"

"God, Mom," he almost sobs. "This isn't fair. What you did is awful. What about Amelia Malone's family? Don't they deserve justice? To know their son is alive?"

What's this? He isn't telling her he already met the Malones?

"Dan, you don't understand," she argues. "That family...they're different. You don't know what kind of people they are. I had to save you from them. It's best if you stay as far away from them as possible."

"Why?" he asks. "They didn't do anything to you. Don't they deserve the chance to know me and me to know them?"

"Daniel, stay away from them!" she shouts, frustrated. "I've worked too hard to keep you safe all these years to have you throw it all away out of a sense of misplaced justice."

"Misplaced?" he asks in disbelief. "You murdered a wife, a mother, and stole her child! How is it misplaced to want them to know the truth?"

"Everyone thinks she died in a car accident," she says wearily. "Let it be, Dan. Come home, and we'll talk about it."

"What about Mattie, Mom?" he asks, instead of answering her plea to come home. "You and Claire took her from her parents too. Who are they? Who are her parents?"

"That girl," Mrs. Richards snarls. "I knew she was going to be trouble. I begged Amanda to leave her alone, but she wouldn't, and look where it got my sister! She's dead because of that girl."

It's so strange to hear Mrs. Richards call my mom Amanda. I know that's her name, but to me she's Claire Hathaway.

"Your sister tried to kill Mattie!" Dan says, shocked. "How is it Mattie's fault she's dead?"

"I knew she'd be the death of Amanda," Mrs. Richards says. "Bad blood, that one. My sister wouldn't be dead now if she hadn't taken that girl and run. It followed her all her days, until she gave in and tried to keep her safe the only way she knew how. If she was dead, Mattie would be safe from herself and her family. I should have known Amanda would kill herself. I should have stopped her, should have refused to help her."

Mrs. Richards is crying. I can tell how much she loved her sister, and I hear the anger and rage directed at me. At least now I understand why she dislikes me so much. It has nothing to do with me being a "violent child," but because she blames me for her sister's death. Just proves what I've always thought. I'm a walking disaster, dangerous to anyone who gets near me. My screwed up life always spills over and causes problems for everybody else.

"Mom, what your sister did is not Mattie's fault," Dan says quietly. "She was only five years old. You can't blame her for your sister's decisions."

Mrs. Richards sighs. "Dan, please just come home, and we'll talk about this."

"I can't, Mom," he says. "Who are her parents?"

There is silence on the other end.

"Who are they?" he demands. "She has a right to know who her family is!"

"Dan, the people I saved you from are…dangerous, but her father, he's a monster. No matter what she's suffered in foster care, it can't compare to what those people could do to her."

"Who, Mom?" Dan's voice has gone hard, cold. He sounds so grown up. "I want a name."

"I can't, Dan," she whispers. "I promised Amanda I'd keep her daughter safe…"

"How would your sister feel knowing you let her daughter grow up in one abusive foster home after another, left her all alone in the hospital after she'd been attacked and left for dead? What would she say to you?"

"You don't understand. That girl, she's different, she's a monster…"

I flinch and catch my breath.

"How dare you!" Dan's voice is soft, silky, deadly. "She's a monster? What did she ever do but try to survive? You're the monster here for what you let happen to her. You knew who she was, and yet you ignored her. Now tell me, Mother, *who is she*?"

"I won't…"

"Give me a name."

I have a feeling they're at a Mexican stand-off, neither willing to budge.

"I can't believe you're being this selfish," Dan says, disgusted. "I've been agonizing over whether to call and warn you all day."

"Warn me?" she asks, alarmed.

"I already talked to the Malones," he says. "I

didn't know if I should warn you or not. Mr. Malone hasn't done anything yet, but his sons might turn you in. They may already have, and do you know who told me to call you, to warn you because you're my mom and you love me? The girl you're calling a monster. She hasn't tried to call the cops. She's told me all day that it doesn't matter what you did, that you're my mom, and no matter what, you love me and I love you. *She* told me to call and warn you so you could get away because she knows how much I love you. That's the girl you're refusing to help. She's the only one fighting for you right now because you're my mom!"

She's very quiet after Dan's outburst, but it did bring Caleb barreling into the room. He must have heard Dan shouting. He looks from me to the phone, and his eyes widen. He understands what's going on. He doesn't look mad or anything, just resigned. Maybe he put himself in Dan's shoes, but he's not staring holes into Dan like Eli's been doing.

"A name, give me a name. She deserves that much for trying to help you after you did nothing but abandon her to one awful hellhole after another."

"I'm so sorry," she says softly. "Please, Dan, don't do this, don't make me do this."

"Now."

I don't have to look at him to know he has his cop face on. Caleb looks impressed.

"Ezekiel. Her father's name is Ezekiel Crane."

"Thank you," Dan whispers. "Now, go upstairs, pack a bag, and get out. Run, run as far and as fast as you can. You know I have to report this, so please don't be there when they come. Please, Mama, just run."

Caleb lets out a long breath and closes his eyes. The woman who murdered his mother is on the other end of the phone, and his brother is telling her to run.

"It's too late," he tells Dan.

We hear a muffled pounding on a door, and I squeeze my arms around Dan as hard as I can. Oh, no. They didn't.

"Oh, God, Dan," she breathes. "They're at the door."

"I'm sorry, Mama." Tears are falling on my hands where they are wrapped around him. His voice is hoarse. "I'll be on the first flight out in the morning."

"I love you so much." She's crying, and it makes a sob rip from Dan.

"I love you too, Mama."

The phone disconnects, and Dan falls forward, his body shaking from the sobs. Caleb lets himself back out, and I sit there, holding him.

I can't even promise it's going to be okay.

It's never going to be okay for him again.

Chapter Seventeen

Caleb is snoozing in the chair, and Dan is passed out on the bed. I wish I could pass out like the dead too, but sleep eludes me. The events of the last few days have caught up to me, and my mind is racing a hundred miles a second. I have so many questions and…I *know my father's name*. I can't believe it. Ever since I can remember, I've dreamed about my dad. When I was a little girl, I'd imagine he'd come rescue me, and we'd all live happily ever after. Those dreams died the older I became.

I always thought my dad abandoned us, walked out and never looked back. Mom never talked about him, so I assumed it hurt too much for her to speak of him. She'd left nothing to tell the Department of Social Services where to even start looking for him. Not a name or an address or a phone number. Now I understand why; she kidnapped me.

Dan mutters something and pulls my hand closer. He hasn't let go of it for hours. He fell asleep clutching it, and I haven't had the heart to pull it away from him. He's the only person I'm comfortable enough with looking at them. My hands are still a little disfigured with pins that help to reshape the shattered bones. Scars crisscross them. The hammer Mrs. Olson used not only shattered bone, but skin and muscle as well. I'll have scars for the rest of my life.

The silence is killing me. I need to be up and moving so my thoughts don't drown me. Everyone agreed that I shouldn't go anywhere by myself, but *I* never agreed to it. Sure, there's some demon out for blood and a house full of ghosts that want to hurt me, but when is that anything new in my crazy, messed up life?

I gently pull my hand from Dan's death grip and slide off the bed. Neither Caleb nor Dan awaken. The floorboards don't creak, and the door doesn't squeak when I open it. No one is in the hallway, and I softly close the door behind me. I need time alone to think. I haven't had that since the morning of the Dan and Meg incident. The plane doesn't count because I was so freaked out I couldn't calm down or relax.

It's freezing out here, I realize. I'm barefoot, so the floorboards are like ice. Doc said his friend experienced a lot of ghost activity on the second floor. Looking around, I don't see anything obvious that screams ghost. Am I seriously considering going looking for the ghosts? Maybe. There was so much pain here, so many trapped souls screaming at me to stay away. Ever since embracing my abilities, the need to help the little buggers has grown exponentially. So not me. I keep trying to squelch the urge, but it keeps rearing its ugly head.

The door at the far end of the hall slowly creaks open. I take a step toward it automatically then pause. I've watched enough scary movies and slasher flicks to know better than to be the stupid chick who goes to check out the strange noise. I've sat in theaters and yelled at those girls. Seriously, it's the lamest thing in the world to go looking for the *why* in a haunted house. I know better.

Do I go or do I run like a girl? Taking a deep breath, I start to walk. I know it's crazy stupid, but the little voice inside dares me to go into the room. When I'm about six inches from the door, it slams closed, and I jump backward at least a foot. Wasn't expecting that. Maybe it's time to run like a girl.

Instead, I force myself back to the door and listen. Scratching. I hear scratching. I put my ear to the door and listen. It's louder this time, level with my ear. Whatever is in there is listening to me too. I know it as well as I know Meg would never be caught dead in a knock-off. There's something in there, and it's daring me to come in.

Do I want to? Yes. I have a newfound respect for all those dumb girls who go off looking for the strange noise. It's hard to walk away from it. You just need to know.

The temperature in the hallway has dropped to below freezing. The hum starts in my ears, like a thousand whispers all talking at once. My ear is still pressed to the door when someone on the other side starts to knock. I jerk away and take a few steps back.

Giggles sound to my left, and I turn to look, but see nothing. Footsteps pound up and down the stairs. The hallway lights dim and flicker. *Don't go out, don't go out, don't go out*, I beg. I *hate* the dark anymore. Bad things happen in the dark.

The lights flicker once more and die, plunging me into total darkness. I blink several times, trying to force my eyes to adjust to the utter black surrounding me. Just flippin' great.

The footsteps start up the stairs again, but they don't go back down. These are heavier than before. It was kids before, but not now. The footsteps keep coming once they hit the landing. They echo closer, and I realize they are coming toward me.

The door in front of me creaks open.

I'm trapped between the two of them. There's nowhere to go.

I swallow hard, hearing the footsteps come to a stop beside me. Ice settles into my bones. It hurts. They ache and scream in protest. The whispers are gone except for one. I close my eyes and focus on it, listening, telling myself over and over that I will hear it.

"Little girls shouldn't be out of bed all alone…"

My eyes pop open. I heard that. Clear as day.

"Who are you?" I whisper the question in my mind.

"Someone who punishes children for disobeying the rules."

"Did you grab me before?"

He laughs. *"No, but had I seen you, I would have. Come into my room, little girl. Let me show you what happens when you disobey."*

Uh, no, not gonna happen. *"I don't think so."*

The cold intensifies, and it burns its way through

me. The ghost standing beside me takes another step toward me, and I shudder, trying hard not to run screaming down the hall. I'm not sure what will happen if I run, and I don't want to know, either.

Instead, I turn my head slightly, and much to my surprise, I can see the ghost standing beside me. He is a large man, heavy set and wearing overalls like a farmer. He's swinging an axe back and forth. It drips blood, spraying the dark substance as it swings. I swallow. His gray eyes are flat, empty, and cold. The malice emanating from him eats at me. He enjoys hurting people.

The ghost standing in front of me causes me to shrink back against the wall as far as I can get. He's shrouded in darkness, but his eyes—his eyes I can see clearly. They are bright, shining with glee. It isn't anger or rage that comes from him. I've never felt anything like it except for once. My mind thinks back to the dream I had in Dan's place, the one where I woke up with my wrist bleeding. The man in that dream exuded the same kind of…evil that this one does. It terrifies me.

He leans closer and sniffs. The smile that lights his face makes me cringe. *"You smell good, girlie. So much energy…I will feast on you for days."*

"Who are you?" I ask again. *"Did you live here before?"* Maybe if I can get him to talk, I can figure out how to escape without causing myself any harm.

His finger runs down my cheek. I gag at the stench of rot. He smells like my old ninth grade science experiment where I recorded the rate of decomposition of a piece of meat left out in the sun.

"Should I let Mikey here have at you first?" he whispers against my cheek, his breath foul. *"He has been so patient, waiting for someone like you. Do you know why that is, little girl?"*

I shake my head, unable to answer. Fear is beginning to spiral out of from the center of my stomach and spread through me.

"You smell of the void, the Between. Your light shines as bright as the light of Heaven. Mikey, here, he needs that light to live, to sustain himself." He leans into me, and I want to scream, but I can't. *"You are a piece of the divine, gone and come again. Your energy can sustain us both for a millennium."*

"That's what you do?" I ask snidely. Fear has always makes me react badly. I go on the offensive and usually say things I shouldn't. *"Go around snacking on little girls like a perv? You're nothing but a coward."*

"Hmm," he whispers. *"You need to learn some respect, little girl. By the time we're done with you, you'll be begging for mercy, and I won't have any. You'll be here forever with us, feeding us."*

"Yeah, about that…never gonna happen, creep. I don't do old pervy men."

He laughs, and it hurts my ears. His hands stroke my bare arms, and I shudder in revulsion. It only makes him chuckle.

"Why am I not surprised you're out here by yourself?"

I turn my head and see Eli glaring at me as he advances, his sword in hand. The ghosts take one look at him and vanish. I slide down the wall, my legs giving out. I have never been so glad to see someone in my entire life.

"What are you doing up so late?" I ask when he sits down beside me.

"I was on monitor duty," he says. "I saw you up here, and then the equipment went crazy. Figured I should come see what kind of trouble you'd gotten yourself into."

"Did you see them?" I ask, shivering at the memory of his hands on me.

He nods and switches the blade back and forth in his hands. It's a telling movement. He was worried, is worried, and trying hard not to show it.

"Why were you talking to them?" he asks. "It was a foolish thing to do."

"Ghosts always talk to me." I shrug. "Could you hear what we were saying?"

"No." He shifts closer to me. "You were talking out loud though, so I could guess. Pervy old man, huh?"

I smile and shake my head. I really should learn to control my mouth. The ghost might have done some real damage if Eli hadn't come along.

"How do you kill them?" I ask. Those two need to pass over to what awaits them. I so hope they end up down under suffering the same fate as they've caused so many others.

"You have to salt and burn the bones to really kill them," Eli tells me. "The sword will do it as well. It's a holy blade, supposedly blessed by God himself."

"You sound as if you doubt that," I say, hearing the sarcasm at the end of his statement.

"Not sure I believe in the whole God thing." He shrugs. "I've seen too much to believe someone up there gives a damn."

I know he has a point. When I look back at all the bad times in my life, at all I've suffered, I sometimes wonder the same thing, but I can never convince myself that there *isn't* someone up there. Maybe it's because of all the bad things that happened in my life that I believe. My old Sunday school teacher once said God only throws things at you he knows you can survive, that what doesn't kill you only makes you stronger. I believed it then, and I still do. I know He's there, even if I don't see Him. Faith. No matter what's happened in my life, I've never lost my faith. I might have learned to rely on my own ingenuity instead of depending upon the divine, but I believe in a higher power. Call it God or whatever you want, but I believe in it. Always will.

"What, not going to try to convince me otherwise?" Eli asks after a minute.

"Nope," I say and stand up. "If you don't believe, there's no point in buggering you about it. Everyone is entitled to his own beliefs."

"I wish Caleb and Dad would leave me alone about it," he says darkly before standing himself. "They think I should just accept that we come from Angels and are on some kind of epic holy mission to fight the battle between heaven and hell."

"So, what do you believe?"

He shrugs. "You'll laugh."

"Ghost Girl, here," I say and point to myself. "Trust me, I won't laugh."

He smiles, and I can't breathe. His whole face lights up when he smiles, and that queasy feeling starts in my stomach again.

"I think we're like the X-Men, genetically mutated or something so we can see things on a different plane of existence than other humans can."

Such a guy thing to say. I bite back a laugh. What guy wouldn't want to be a superhero with powers to save the world?

"So which X-Man would you be?" I ask.

"Wolverine, of course." He looks at me as if to say, 'well, duh.'

"I like Storm. She has some wicked abilities, much better than mine."

"I'll give you Storm," he agrees. "Halle Berry was hot in that movie, and she kicked ass."

I roll my eyes. Leave it to Eli to go straight to the hot chick scenario and forget all about Storm's ability to control the elements.

"So, Mattie, what do you think causes us to be the way we are?"

I shrug. I have no idea. "Who knows?"

"Do you buy into the whole God thing and the greater purpose?"

"I think that we all have free will to make our own choices, Eli, but yeah, I do believe in the whole God thing."

"Why?" His face is a mask of curiosity as he stares down at me. I feel tiny next to him. He towers over me, even sitting. "From what the doc said, you've had a pretty crappy life. How can you believe in a God after everything you've been through?"

"Did you ever just know something, Eli? You couldn't explain it or maybe even understand it, but you knew it deep in your gut?"

He nods slowly.

"That's how I know God's there. Yeah, I've had a pretty bad life, but there have been good spots in it too. I met my social worker, who cares what happens to me. I met Dan and his dad, who taught me that I'm worth something, and I met Mary and her mom. They gave me a home, knowing what I can do and not caring. As many bad things as have happened to me, I've been given gifts too. Even I'm not so screwed up that I don't realize a blessing when I get one."

"So, you really believe there's this being bigger than life watching over us?"

"Yup."

"Hmm…"

"I guess I should get back to my room," I say after a few minutes.

"Yeah, I guess you should," he agrees, but neither of us moves.

His eyes are glowing in the dark, the aqua color mesmerizing. There's almost a light shining out of them. Looking into those eyes, I firmly believe he's been blessed by God, even if he doesn't. He can only see evil, but I can see everything, and there's nothing but a pure goodness living inside him. He can be a complete jerk at times, but he has the light of Heaven around him.

"Would you hit me again if I kissed you?" he asks, startling me out of my thoughts.

"Probably," I tell him.

"I think it might be worth another black eye," he muses and leans closer.

My heartrate speeds up and my breath catches. I've been wondering all day what it would feel like if he kissed me. Just the thought has me near hyperventilation. I've never ever in my life reacted this strongly to anyone, ever.

His breath whispers across my face, and the queasy feeling intensifies. Maybe this is not such a good idea.

"I wouldn't," I blurt out, embarrassed.

"Why not?" he asks, pushing me against the wall with his body.

"Being this near you...it, uh...it makes me a little sick to my stomach," I confess unhappily, my face ten shades of crimson.

Much to my chagrin, he laughs. "That's a *good* thing, Mattie."

"My wanting to barf all over you is a good thing?" I ask, flummoxed. Is he insane?

"Let me show you why it's a good thing," he breathes, and before I can guess what he's about, his lips are on mine.

Fire explodes through my entire body. The queasy feelings go away and are replaced by the strongest sense of need I've ever felt. I want him closer, need him like I need air to breathe. My fingers twist in his hair, and I pull him to me, my lips softening, giving in to this demand of his.

Eli deepens the kiss, and for a few minutes we are both lost to feelings that overwhelm us. He groans and pulls away, his forehead resting on mine. His eyes are bright and dark at the same time.

My ragged breathing matches his.

"Understand now?" he whispers.

Um, yeah, I do. I used to read the romance novels my foster moms would leave lying around. I read all about the desire that flared up between people. That's what this is I feel around him. Desire. Not sure if I like it or not. It's intense.

"I've wanted to do that since I met you," he confesses.

"Even though I hit you twice?"

He laughs, his smile contagious. "Maybe not in those moments, but yeah, even though you hit me, Hilda."

"Call me Hilda one more time, and I really will hit you again," I threaten half-heartedly. It's hard to stay mad at him when he smiles.

"Come on." He grabs my hand and starts leading me down the hall. "I'll walk you to your room."

"What if I don't want to go back to my room?"

He stops and turns toward me. "What do you want to do?"

The ice creeps back up my spine, and I stiffen, looking. We're in the center of the hallway. Eli takes a step toward me, his sword swinging up at the ready.

Every door in the hallway flies open and slams shut, causing me to let out a startled scream.

That's when I see him.

Standing at the end of the hallway, the man from the porch is staring at me. His eyes are harsh, hollow. I am exactly where he wanted me to be, in the house. With him.

He smiles.

Chapter Eighteen

"Boys!"

Mr. Malone comes barreling up the stairs about the same time Dan and Caleb race out of my room. They all come face to face with the man from the porch.

"Mattie, you okay?" Dan asks me, a frown on his face when he notices I'm shoulder to shoulder with Eli.

"Fine," I tell him, never taking my eyes off the man at the end of the hallway. When Caleb goes to flip the light switch, I stop him. "Don't, Caleb. Leave the lights off." I'm not sure why, but I know turning the lights on will cause him to leave and I want to know why he's so eager to get me in this house.

The man cocks his head and looks at me, his gaze assessing. He's dressed in a black suit and my mind immediately goes to *Poltergeist* with a twist of *Phantasm*. I watch way too many scary movies.

"Who are you?" I ask him.

"This is my home," he replies. *"Who are you?"*

"This isn't your home anymore," I tell him softly. "You're dead."

"Yes," he agrees. *"It's a very unfortunate state of affairs, isn't it?"*

"Mattie, I don't think it's a good idea to talk to it," Dan whispers in my ear. I hadn't heard him move up behind me, but then I am a little preoccupied.

I give him my best exasperated look. True, this ghost scares the bejeezus out of me, but if I can talk to it, I might figure out what it wants from me. "He's not an it, Officer Dan. He's just a lost soul who needs some help."

The ghost bursts out laughing. I glare at him, which only makes him laugh harder.

"Squirt, *I* can see it, which means it's not the type of ghost you're used to. That thing is not lost or in need of help. It's something that has been warped and twisted, something that hurts others because it likes to."

"Your beau is right about that, young one," the ghost wheezes. *"I love to hurt others. Always have."*

I can hear his intent to hurt me in his tone and I'm ever so glad no one else here can. They wouldn't let me try to talk to him if they could. I need to understand why I'm so important to him. Even now, when I feel all his glee at the thought of causing me pain, I can feel his need to have me here. It's very confusing.

"He's not my beau," I reply, switching to an internal chat so no one else can hear what we're saying. Dan is a lot of things to me, but my beau he

isn't. Nor does he want to be. He chose Meg. It was *easy* with her. That still stings, I realize. More than stings, it hurts down to depths of my soul. I can't dwell on it now though, so I push it aside. *"Why do you want me here?"*

The ghost sighs. He looks much older than he had when I first saw him on the porch upon my arrival.

"You are special, girl. There are only a handful of people with abilities even close to your own, but none quite like you. I felt you when you entered the city, knew you were on your way to me. With you, I can cement my control over all of them."

"What do you mean?" I ask.

"My souls, they have been growing stronger over the decades, some almost as strong as I am. I will not lose control of them, child. Your soul will give me the power I need for an eternity. Your light will feed me until I grow so strong, nothing can hurt me."

I take a step back at the malice and determination in his voice. Dan is a solid wall at my back and I lean into him. The ghost in front of me is like nothing I've ever felt before. It's so sure of itself. Most ghosts are lost, unable to move on because they either don't realize they're dead or plain old refuse to admit the fact of their demise. This one relishes being dead, he loves the power he gains from the souls around him. It's disturbing.

"You okay?" Dan whispers.

I nod, even though I'm not. Being in this ghost's presence is draining. He saps all the energy out of me from over a hundred feet away.

"Can we just kill it?" Eli asks, his voice bored. "Why talk to it?"

"This is her thing, let her do it," Dan tells him, his voice sharp. I roll my eyes. He'd asked me why I was talking to it not five minutes ago.

"That little stick of his can't hurt me," the ghost whispers.

"He says it can," I counter.

"Let him try," the ghost smirks. *"You need to understand that no one can save you from me."*

"He says your sword can't hurt him," I tell Eli hesitantly. I'm not too sure I want Eli anywhere near him.

"Really?" Eli laughs and saunters toward the ghost. The man grins wider, but doesn't move as Eli swings…and swings…and swings. The sword slashes again and again, but to no avail. Eli stares at the man, dumbfounded. I can sympathize. It's how I'm feeling right now. If a holy blade can't kill it, how can we hope to?

The man laughs and suddenly Eli is airborne, flying backward. He crashes into me and Dan. We all go tumbling backward. I frantically try to free myself from the mass of limbs, but Eli is too heavy.

I blink and the man is crouched down in front of me. His blue eyes are hard, a killer's eyes. He traces his hand down my cheek and I shudder. His touch freezes the blood in my body, my bones scream in protest. My teeth start to chatter and I push backward, but Eli is completely unconscious on top of me. Dan is working to push himself up, but I can't help. The ghost in front of me has all my attention.

"You see, girl, there's nothing you can do to stop me. Before this night is out, I will have you." He stands up and looks over to where Caleb and Mr. Malone are standing. *"Tell them to leave this place now and I will spare all of them. You're the only one I want."*

With that he vanishes.

Chapter Nineteen

I stare at the room Eli picked for himself. The walls are a dark gold and the furniture all dark mahogany wood. The bed clothes are done in shades of cream and chocolate. It's a very masculine room. It also has its own en suite. Leave it to Eli to find one of the few rooms with its own bathroom.

The boy in question lay on his bed, unconscious. His father and Caleb had moved him here and then they'd gone back out into the hallway to argue about the best course of action. Doc had finally showed up as well. He said he'd been watching from the control room and had gotten all sorts of readings. Here we'd all been facing a possible hostile situation and he'd been recording data. I know I shouldn't be surprised, but I thought he'd have at least been concerned enough about me to come help.

As kind as Doctor Olivet has been to me, I guess he's like everyone else. When it comes right down to it, it's all about him. Never mind anyone else.

167

I laugh at my own bitter statement. Over the last couple months, I've grown completely jaded and bitter. I know it and so does everyone around me. I can't help it. After everything I've been through, I have every right to a good sulk. Even Dan turned out to be less than the perfect guy I thought him to be. Why can no one ever put me first? Why can't I have someone care about me so much the only thing that matters to them is me? I just want someone to love me like that and I don't think I'll ever have it.

How very maudlin I sound tonight. Eli mutters something and I turn my attention back to him. He is quite possibly the most beautiful person I've ever seen. A guy would never take kindly to being called beautiful, but that's the only word I have to describe him. He looks very young too, with his face relaxed. There's a tiny scar on his chin that should mar his looks, but it only makes him appear all the more beautiful for being flawed. He'd said he didn't believe they carried an angel's blood in them, but looking at him right now, I do.

My fingertips feather over my lips remembering the kiss he and I shared before the ghost showed up and ruined the moment. I'm not sure if I'm angrier about the interruption or his wanting to eat my soul. Not only am I maudlin, I'm sounding even more fickle than I usually do. This house and yes, even Eli, are doing strange things to me, making me feel things I normally wouldn't. I'm tired, too. I think the soul sucker ghost is feeding off me already and I don't have a clue as to how to stop it. Maybe that's why I'm suddenly in this odd mood.

The light from the bathroom bathes the room in a

soft glow. I'd told Mr. Malone to leave the bedroom lights off so that when Eli woke up, he wouldn't be blinded. Caleb had switched on the bathroom light instead. He didn't want us in the dark. Who can blame him after everything that's happened tonight? I know I should be more alarmed at everything, but I can't. I feel detached, morose.

"Emma Rose…"

My head snaps up. Where did that come from? It's not even cold…yes it is, I'm so cold already I hadn't noticed it. The light in the bathroom has dimmed and I can hear the water dripping. When did that start?

"Who's there?" I ask, feeling no fear, only a sense of the inevitable.

All I can hear is the drip, drip, drip of the faucet.

The bathroom door widens, an open invitation to enter. Why not, I think. It's not like I'm going to survive the night anyway. I'm ghost food one way or another. Why not tempt fate?

Standing up, the first thing I notice is that I'm not really standing. I'm fast asleep in the chair beside Eli's bed. If I weren't in such a weird mood, I might actually be freaked, but as it is, it's a curiosity and nothing more.

The bathroom is the same studio from my dream and the painter is muttering something as he works. The familiar scent of blood wraps around me as I move into the room. His work is still morbid but it's also beautiful. The art inspires emotions. The haunting look captured in the eyes of the models moves you to feel pain, fear, and grief. He's grieving, I realize. That's why his paintings are so

169

dark and full of pain. They're a reflection of him.

"Hello?" I call out, not wanting to startle him. I know what it feels like to ruin a perfectly good painting or drawing because one brush stroke ran awry.

"There's something not right about it," he says. *"What do you think, Emma? What's missing?"*

"My name is Mattie," I tell him, but step closer to look at his work. The woman looks lost, alone, and totally heartbroken. Her face screams pain, but not a physical one. It's the pain of grief, of loss. He's right though, something's missing. It lacks the life of the painting I'd seen before. There is no heart, no soul in this one. It's dark and terrifying, but you can dismiss that. You couldn't before. His other work kept your eyes on the painting, your heart racing.

"There's no life in it," I tell him. "She's in pain, but you can't feel it as deeply when you look at it like you could your others."

"Oui, cherie!" he nods. *"I knew you would see what I see. Do you understand why it is so?"*

I shake my head no.

He points to the table behind him. The sheet covering his latest victim is sticky and blotched with old blood stains.

"Her life gave out before I could finish it, but it was a little dull even before her soul finally left. Do you remember my last one? It glowed with life, with emotion. Can you guess why?"

"I don't know."

"You, Emma Rose. You did that. It was your blood, your soul that gave that painting life. Just a

few drops and you can give this one life."

He has my hand again and his knife is slashing. I flinch at the pain, but stare transfixed as he catches a bit of the blood and then rushes to the painting. Only a few strokes and the image on the canvas starts to breathe. It becomes vibrant, real, and the emotions so strong, it almost drives me to my knees.

"You see, cherie," he coos. *"Look at what your blood did. Come, let me show you more."* He holds out his hand to me and I'm so tempted to take it but I don't know why. His eyes are still that dark bloody black of a demon's, but I want to go to him so badly.

"I…I can't."

"Of course you can, Emma Rose," he smiles. *"You need my help."*

"What?" I ask, startled. His help?

He crosses the gap between us and takes both my hands.

I scream from the pain. Cold…so cold. It feels as if my bones have turned to ice and the air in my lungs freeze up. The cold is so intense it burns and I look down to see my legs are encased in ice again. I can't move.

"Shh, poppet," he whispers. *"The pain is nothing but a tool. Use it. Use the pain to fight. You have to fight, Emma."*

"Fight?" I force the word out of frozen lips. It hurts so much.

"You're dying, Emma, right now. If you don't fight, there is no hope. Your soul is being drained and you're not fighting."

"I don't want to fight," I whisper. And I didn't. What was the point? Nothing good ever happens to me. Why not just die and be done with it?

"What is wrong with you, Emma Rose? This is not who you are. You always fight."

"That's the point," I shout, forgetting the pain for a moment. "All I ever do is fight and what good has it done me? Where has fighting ever gotten me? I have nothing and no one. I can't even draw anymore." I lift up my hands. "Why fight when I can't do what I love? When I can't trust anyone?"

"Trust me, poppet," he says. *"If you die here, you will be trapped with all of them, feeding him for an eternity. You don't know pain until you've felt your soul ripped from you, saw it eaten, and then have to go on with this hollow feeling. Don't lose yours, Emma Rose, not yet."*

"Who are you?" I ask again, disturbed that this madman is concerned about me.

"It doesn't matter," he says. His eyes, usually full of madness and evil, shines with something akin to sorrow tonight. *"What matters is that you wake up and fight."*

"But why?" I ask. "Why do you care?"

"Because you're mine, Emma Rose, and I will be the one to kill you. No one else. Do you understand me? Wake up, girl, and fight!"

Hands are shaking me and I struggle against them. The pain is back and it's all I can do to breathe.

"Mattie, please wake up."

I can hear Dan, but his voice is faint, like he's very far away. My entire body is shaking from the cold. I've never been this cold before.

"We need to get her warm," another voice argues. "What the...why is she bleeding?"

"Oh God," Dan whispers close to my ear. "She's dreaming again. It has to be the same dream..."

"What are you talking about?" I feel Eli's warm breath on my face. When did he wake up?

"Right before she came here, she had a dream about a guy who cut her wrist. When she woke up, her wrist was bleeding. Where's she bleeding?"

"Her wrist," Eli says, confusion in his voice. "Caleb, get me something to stop this blood."

My eyes open and all I see is a world of aqua. His beautiful eyes are full of fear and worry.

"Mattie?" he whispers. "Can you hear me?"

"She's awake?" Dan demands. "Squirt? You okay?"

I'm too tired to answer either of them. Why am I so tired?

Then I see him. He's standing in the corner, unnoticed by anyone else. He's grinning, but he looks younger than he did before. He looks alive and his eyes are glowing a rich blue. It's my soul that's making those eyes glow. The old man is feasting on my soul.

He's killing me just like he said he would.

Chapter Twenty

"I can't leave you alone for even a few days, can I?"

I force my head to turn slightly. He's standing in the doorway with an irritated look on his face. Eric.

"Eric?" I whisper. "What are you doing here?"

"Eric?" Dan asks. "Where's Eric?"

"Who's Eric?" Eli demands.

"Saving you again." He sighs and starts toward the man sitting in the corner.

"No," I scream, my voice not as loud as it should be. "Don't go near him!"

Eric stops and looks at the man, really looks at him. His face turns horrified. *"He's...he's...he's consuming your energy, your soul, Mattie."*

"I don't know how to stop him," I say.

"It's more than that." Eric walks over to the bed. *"You don't want to stop him. Why?"*

"Because my life is too hard, Eric. I'm tired. I just want to stop."

"What?" Both Dan and Eli whisper. Even though they can only hear one side of the conversation, both understand what I'm saying. I don't want to fight, to live like this anymore.

"I can't believe you're being this selfish, Mathilda Louise Hathaway," Eric rages at me, his blue eyes so full of anger for a moment they pulse with a light I've never seen. His face starts to contort, to bleed, to rip, to tear, to shred and I'm staring at Mirror Boy once again. That ragged sound of nails screaming as they are sawed in two hammers at me. I remember in this instant why he terrified me.

Caleb and his dad draw their swords and Eli slides off the bed, drawing his own. Dan sits up and gapes at the image before him. He tries to drag me to the other side of the bed, but I won't go. Weak as I am, I won't run from Eric. Never again.

"Don't you dare touch a hair on his head," I warn Eli and struggle to sit up.

"Get back, Mattie," he warns me. "You don't know what this is…"

"I know perfectly well what he is," I rebuff and try to stand but end up falling to the floor. I'm too weak. Dan is there, though, yanking me up. "It's Eric."

"That is not Eric," Dan denies. "It can't be Eric."

"Dan, meet Mirror Boy," I say softly. "I'm not selfish, Eric. No matter what you think, I'm not selfish."

"Yes, Mattie, you are selfish," he yells and I flinch at the pain that shoots through my head. *"After everything we did to save you, you'd throw it all away?"*

"Eric, please," I beg, switching to my internal

chat. *"Don't be mad. You said you'd wait for me and I'm ready to go. If I'm here, we can't ever be together, but if I die, you and I can go, we can cross over and forget about all the pain we've suffered. We can be happy."*

"Even if that's true, Mattie, I'd never let you do it," he tells me. *"You mean too much to me. I want you to live like every day is your last day. You deserve to be happy, to fall in love, to have children and be the mom you wanted yours to be. Live Mattie, please don't give up."*

I turn away at the raw emotion in his voice, in his eyes, and bury my face in Dan's chest as I've done so often over the last months. No matter what Eric's face looks like, his eyes are always the same. He did work hard to save me. Am I throwing that gift away? That blessing? I'm so tired and my heart hurts so much.

"Mattie, you are the only girl I'll ever love this side of the veil," Eric whispers, *"but it can never be. You know this, I know this. You're hurting right now. I know you feel raw and ragged, like your heart has been shattered into a thousand pieces. You're angry at everyone and everything. You feel like you've lost everything good in your life, but that's not true."*

"It is true," I say, tears trailing wet paths down my cheeks. "I lost Dan. He may not know it yet, but we can't survive what's coming. He'll never forgive me."

"What are you talking about, Mattie?" Dan asks. "You haven't done anything."

"I did," I nod, not looking at any of them. "I

asked you to find my family and it cost you yours. I destroyed everything good in your life. If you'd never met me, you and your mom and dad and brother would still be a happy family. You wouldn't be seeing ghosts or demons. You'd just be the nice guy who always tries to do the right thing."

Dan forces my chin up so that I'm looking at him. "Mattie, none of this is your fault and I would *never* blame you for any of it. Why would you even think that?"

"Because everything I care about is taken away, destroyed, and it's always my fault. I always do something to wreck everything good in my life. I just never thought I'd do such a bang-up job with you. I never meant to hurt you."

"Squirt, don't," Dan soothes. "Please don't cry. I swear to you, this isn't your fault. You only wanted to find out where you came from. No one expected this to happen. If anybody is to blame, it's my mom and your mom. If they'd thought about the consequences of what they were doing, none of this would be happening."

"Stop whining, Mattie," Eric tells me harshly. *"You've been droning on and on about all the bad things for as long as I've known you. This pity train of yours is starting to get boring."*

"Boring?" I screech and turn around, intending to launch myself at him. How dare he say that to me? It's not his life, it's mine. Dan catches me before I fall. God, I wish I wasn't so weak.

"Yeah, boring," he nods, his face starting to melt back to its cute self. *"Sure, you've had a pretty bad life, had terrible things happen to you, but you need*

to get over it, get over yourself. You're surrounded by people who love you, who would do anything for you, and you refuse to accept it. You see it, but you won't reach out and grab it. Instead you focus on the bad stuff and not the good."

"What do I have that's so good?"

"You have a home now, with people who love you and accept that you're different. Mary and her mom would do anything for you. You're family to them. Dan is family, even the Malones here will be your family if you let them. You only have to snap out of this depression that thing in the corner has put you in and fight for it—fight, Mattie."

"I don't know if I can."

"If you won't fight for yourself, then fight for me, the same way I fought for you. Fight for Dan, fight for the chance at love with the guy glowering at me. I've seen your future, Mattie, seen where it takes you. It's dark and deadly, but there is this shining beacon of love on two paths. Either path will make you happy. You just have to fight for the chance."

I close my eyes at the pain his voice brings. His face may be normal, but his voice is still eating away at my head. It hurts.

"Can't you feel the pain and suffering in this house, Mattie?" Eric queries softly. *"All these souls crying out for help. If you die, you stay here with them, become one of those souls crying out for help, trapped forever with the monster who will use you to hurt them. Who will save them if you don't?"*

Their pain has been battering me since I crossed the property line. My goal when I felt it was to help them cross over, end their pain. That was always my endgame, but somehow I got derailed. I frown, thinking. When did that stop being important to me?

It stopped when I woke up from being unconscious, I realize. I turn my attention to the ghost in the corner. He'd started to feed on me while I was out. He'd worn my spirit down and it had suffered so much, all the new emotional pain that I'd been going through magnified, making me think there was no way out, no reason to fight.

But I don't quit, I tell myself. I'm a fighter, will always be a fighter, and no one, especially not some creepy old ghost with a God complex is going to take me down. Not today. I'm Mattie Freaking Hathaway and I don't do scared.

But how do I break the hold he has on me?

"How?" I ask Eric. "How can I stop him?"

"You can't kill him," he warns me. *"Not right now. You're too weak, but you can break his hold. You need to take one of the swords."*

"They don't work against him," I say. "Eli tried and nothing happened."

"That's because he doesn't believe, Mattie," Eric says. *"These swords need faith. They need a true believer to work as they were meant to work. Trust me, just pick it up."*

"Eli, give me your sword." I hold out my hand.

Eli balks, refusing to hand it over. "Why?"

"Of for the love of Pete, just give me the danged sword!"

Eli grudgingly comes over. "Are you even strong enough to hold this thing?"

"I am if you help me," I tell him.

He frowns but holds the sword out for me to

grasp. The minute I take it from him my arms are so weak, they fall, the swords pointing down. My blood begins to trickle down my hand and onto the silver of the blade. The sword begins to glow, runes along the surface of the blade lighting up. The light is so bright I use my free hand to shield my eyes. Soon it dims and looks normal again, but it feels different. It feels alive and eager.

"What just happened?" Eli demands.

"Tell him the blade will never fail him again," Eric smiles. *"Tell him it is soaked in the blood of someone who truly believes and will always work against any foe."*

"Eric says your sword will never fail you again," I say softly. "He says it's soaked in the blood of someone who truly believes and that is what it needed to work."

"So he thinks your blood what, fixed it or something?" Eli asks, confused.

"Something like that," I say. "Try it."

"No, Mattie," Eric stops me. *"You have to be the one to break the bond with him. You have to cut him."*

"I have let you have your way long enough, boy," the man snarls from the corner. *"Enough of this. You cannot stop me."*

I glare at the old guy and then blink. He's not so old anymore. He's much, much younger, maybe mid-forties? What the…?

"No, Eli. I have to do this, but you have to help me lift it. I'm not strong enough."

Eli frowns again, but pulls me free of Dan. He wraps an arm around me and hauls me against his side, dragging me closer to the man, who is now standing.

"You do not think it is going to be that easy, do you?" he laughs. I get a sense of what he's going to do, he's going to throw us backward like he did to Eli earlier. Before I can shout a warning, Eric launches himself at the ghost, grappling with him. It's terrifying to behold. I see flashes of color and the room shakes like an earthquake is hitting.

"Now, Mattie!" Eric yells. *"Do it now! I can't hold him for much longer!"*

Together, Eli and I lift up the sword and swing at the ghosts. I hear a hiss and a moan. A gash has opened up along the man's right arm and blue light starts to leak out of him. He howls in pain and throws Eric at us the same time we swing again. My eyes widen in horror, unable to stop the swing, to stop the blade from slicing into Eric. NO!

The man laughs and disappears but Eric falls, his face ashen. Oh, God, no, what have I done?

"Eric," I whisper, falling to my knees beside him. "Please, Eric, please don't die."

"I'm already dead," he chuckles, his voice sounding hollow. *"I need you to do something for me, Mattie."*

"Anything."

"If I die here, that thing will eat my soul," he whispers. *"I don't want that, not ever again. To be trapped in constant pain and terror. Never again."*

"Tell me what to do." He's starting to fade, but there's nothing I can do to stop it.

"I promised I'd wait for you, do you remember?"

I nod, a sob breaking free.

"There's only one way I can keep that promise, one way I can be a part of you forever. You have to take my energy. It's the only way to make you strong enough to fight that thing. You have to consume my soul."

"No! I won't do that. Don't ask me to do that!"

"You can do it," Eric soothes. *"Your gift is so much more than you can imagine, you can do this for me and every other trapped soul here. Let me give you this, Mattie, let me give you the gift of my life."*

"No," I cry, shaking in grief. "Don't ask me to do this, please, Eric."

"Mattie, if you don't do this and do it now, that thing will have me and I'll be lost forever. Don't make me suffer like that. Let me go knowing that I died being the hero and saving the girl I love. Please do this for me, Mattie, please."

"What do I do?" There's no chance I'm ever letting that thing get its hands on Eric. He has saved me so many times, I can do this for him.

"Just touch me, sweetheart, just touch me."

I lay my hand upon his face and electricity jolts up my arm. I watch as Eric fades to a glowing mass of energy, watch as it snakes up my arm and then I scream when all that glowing energy seeps into my skin, into my soul, giving me back life and strength and love. He loved me so much and I feel that as I feel nothing else. This boy loved me the way I'd always wanted to be loved, the way I needed to be loved, and he gave his life for me.

I want to scream and rage at the unfairness of it

all, but I don't. I won't disrespect his memory like that. I will honor him by being the person he thought I was.

I will save them all.

And that old man will die screaming for what he's done.

Chapter Twenty-One

They're all standing in the corner whispering and giving me worried glances. We moved back down to the library after the incident. I guess everyone feels safer here. It's the books. Books always remind you of safety, but I don't know why that is.

It's been over an hour and I haven't said a word to any of them. How can I? I don't want to talk to anyone, don't want to admit any of this is real. I can't cry. Not that I don't want to, I simply can't. I need to cry, but my heart is too numb. How much can one person take?

He can't be gone, my Mirror Boy. He'd saved my life more times than I can count. He'd sat with me while I was dying so I wouldn't be alone and then stayed with me when I didn't die, all so I would never be alone. How can this happen? He's supposed to be here to listen to me rant and then tell me it's all going to be okay. But he's not.

I want him back.

But he can't come back.

It's a fundamental knowledge I can't escape. I

know he can't come back because of who I am, what I'm supposed to do when I become a reaper. For the first time, I understand what it means to reap a soul. It hurts. It isn't a physical pain, but an emotional one. I felt his sadness at leaving me and it made my grief that much harder to bear.

I love Dan, I do, but it's nothing like what I felt for Eric. It's like a piece of me has been ripped away and I can't bear it. I know it's crazy to feel like that about a ghost, but I do. If he'd been alive, we'd have been so happy. He always encouraged me to date, to find someone. He knew we couldn't be together, knew it wasn't a healthy relationship for me, but he never pushed me away, never betrayed me, and was always there for me no matter what. I loved him so much and he's just…gone.

Not able to stand sitting still, I push up off the couch and start to prowl through the books. Everyone pauses and watches me for a minute before going back to their quiet conversation. They're worried about me, especially since Dan and the Doc explained who Eric was to me. They needn't have been. Since we sliced a chunk out of the ghostie, his tie to me has been broken. I'm not feeling depressed and ready to give up anymore. I'm angry, furious, and wanting revenge. Grief is tearing around the edges of those emotions though, and it's all I can do to breathe.

"Here."

I jump, startled at the sound of Eli's voice. He's shoving a knife at me and I cringe.

"I don't want that."

"Look, it's been blessed, same as the swords,

and you need something to protect you."

"You don't understand." I shake my head and step away from the blade. Knives are about the only thing on this plane of existence that scares me. "I can't…not a knife."

"It's only a knife, Mattie." He looks confused.

"I don't like knives," I whisper. "Please put it away."

He does as I ask, but says, "I just wanted you to have something to protect yourself with against the things in this house."

"I know, but not a knife."

"What do you have against knives?"

I shake my head and walk away from him. I'm not in the mood to get into that conversation. Besides, Doc has already spilled enough of my secrets as it is. I don't know these people and I don't want them knowing every little detail about my life.

"Leave her alone for a bit," I hear Dan say.

"I was only trying to help her…"

"I know," Dan tells his brother. "She knows that, but she has a thing about knives. When she learns to trust you, she might tell you, but for right now, just let it be."

Leave it to Dan to swoop in and smooth ruffled feathers even when he himself is living a nightmare. His kindness has always irked me, though. Sometimes he's too bloody nice for his own good. I mean, these boys turned in his mom and here he is trying to placate the one directly responsible. He needs to shout, to scream, to yell. Instead, he's trying to do what he always does and be the good guy.

Before I revert to a classic Mattie move, I walk all the way across the room from them and instead focus on the old books that line the walls. There are several classics, first editions, I'd wager, but I'm afraid to look. Some of them look so fragile, even the thought of touching them makes me afraid they'd shrivel up into dust.

One in particular catches my eye. It looks like an old leather bound journal. Cautiously, I pull it free and gently open it. It is a journal penned by Elizabeth St. John in 1782. The pages look brittle but they aren't. I take my find to one of the couches and sit down to read. Reading about someone else's life might distract me from my own.

1784, May 16

I cannot believe that Father has done this. He signed the contract today to wed me to Mr. Jonas Sinclair, a man that is old enough to be my grandfather. Father said I should be grateful he arranged such a prosperous match for me, but I am devastated.

How can he do this to me? Mother says I am being fickle, that Father worked hard to find me a good husband. A good husband? Mr. Sinclair is sixty-five years of age and I am only fifteen. How can this be a good match?

This year was to be my season of the ton. I was to be presented at my coming out ball. It has been planned for over a year. I have the ball gowns still packed for our trip to London and then today I am informed that it will not transpire, that a match has already been made for me.

What am I to do? I have dreamed of my season since I was a little girl. I wanted to go to the balls, be wooed by all the handsome bachelors and fall in love. Now all that is gone. I am not even to have a grand wedding. Father says it will be a private affair here at our country home. Not only does he deprive me of my season, he will not give me a grand and proper wedding.

Maybe I will wear my best black dress to the wedding in protest.

1784, June 3

I begged and pleaded, but to no avail. I am now a married woman to a husband I despise. There is something about him that scares me. It is the look in his eyes when he stares at me. I have a suspicion that he enjoys pain, and my father just handed me over to him without so much as a second thought.

I was not even given time to say goodbye to my mother after the ceremony before I was hustled away from my home and on board a ship. Our destination is a mystery to me as my new husband did not see fit to share it with me before stealing me away from my home.

Mother refused to speak to me of what is to happen tonight. She said I would get through it. Her advice was to close my eyes and think of something else. She offered no comfort to me, her only child. She did not even see me off when we left. Only our housekeeper bore witness to my departure. None of the other servants could even look at me without pity. Do they know something I do not about my husband? They must if they could only stare at me in pity for the last few weeks.

The ship cast off hours ago, but I have yet to even see my husband. He has abandoned me to our cabin. Perhaps he will fall overboard and I will not have to perform any "wifely duties," as my mother calls it. I have a general idea of what will transpire tonight. I have often eavesdropped on the housemaids chatting about their romps with various men.

I hear footsteps outside our cabin. I dread what is coming even as I know I cannot escape it.

1784, June 4
It was even more awful than I had imagined. Mother's advice did no good. It hurt and my darling husband enjoyed my pain. When I cried, Jonas merely laughed. He told me that he would always do his best to make it as painful for me as possible. I am wed to a cruel man. How could my

parents have done me such a horrid disfavor? They've given me to a man who will spend his years tormenting me. How am I to bear this?

We are heading for a city named New Orleans. Jonas has a home there and assures me there is a higher class of society than the barbaric Americans who live to the north. Creoles, he calls them, a mixture of Spanish and French citizens, have developed a very sophisticated society in the budding city.

Despite his assurances, I am nervous. I have heard so many stories of the wilderness and of the Indians' brutality. The Americans pose a threat as well. They have proven to be quite ruthless in their bid for freedom from Great Britain. Some of the war stories we have been regaled with make me shudder even now.

I am expected to live in an unknown place with no friends or family with a husband who delights in torturing me. How have I ended up here in this place? Did I do something to upset God? Is he punishing me for some unnamed offense?

I wish that I knew.

1784, June 29

We have arrived and the house is beautiful. The architecture is a gorgeous blending of French and Spanish influences. I cannot even begin to describe how breathtaking the mansion is. It's also unsettling. It is hard to properly explain this feeling. Jonas tells me I am being childish and to act like the grown woman I am.

Am I behaving like a child? Everywhere I go, I feel as if I am being watched. There are noises in the house as well. Sometimes I swear I can hear footsteps where there are none. Jonas says it's the house settling. It was built only four years ago and there is still a lot of construction going on. The plantation requires a lot of people to run it and Jonas is building housing for the people who work the fields.

Then there is this atrocious smell that appears at the oddest of times. Its odor is quite foul. The cook has come across it as well and says it smells of rotten eggs. If she can smell it, then surely it can be proven to Jonas? He is adamant in his vocal opinions of my fears. It is of no consequence to him.

Jonas has taken to berating me verbally in front of the staff. It makes me feel so inadequate. Nothing I do is the proper thing. He says I embarrass him in front of his friends with my lack of training in how to run a household and entertain his guests.

I attended the very best finishing schools in France. I know how to flawlessly run a household, but when Jonas begins his tirade, it all escapes me. I feel useless, and worse, the staff are beginning to whisper and laugh at me when they think I am not looking. I am humiliated and all alone.

Jonas refuses to let me attend any functions the women in town hold. He says it is useless nonsense and I would do better idling my time at attempting to learn how to be a proper wife. He allows me to have no friends or companions. When we host parties, he keeps me planted to his side. None of the other women have even attempted friendships with me. They are cold and disdainful. I suspect it is Jonas's doing. What has he told their husbands about me?

I feel dreadfully alone out here, cut off from everyone. Each day becomes harder than the last to believe that I am not as Jonas says I am. He calls me weak, useless, and pathetic. Some days, I believe it myself. How much longer can I go on like this?

1784, July 9
He struck me today. My eye is swollen and black. He struck me.

1784, July 23
Jonas is angry with me as I have not yet begun to increase with his child. He swears that if I am barren he will have me killed and thrown into the swamp. He is serious. I can see the intent in his eyes.

I have done my duties every night and

listened to him laugh as I cried. What more can I do? I cannot force his seed to take root. Nor do I wish to die, either. The cook, Nettie, is my only friend here. I think I shall speak with her on the matter as I have no one else. I understand that ladies are not to form bonds with the help, but as they are all the company Jonas allows, then I will do as I must.

1784, July 28
I am torn asunder. What Nettie suggests is blasphemous, but what choice do I have? He has already beaten me once. If he does it again, I am not sure I can survive it. Jonas enjoys causing me pain, any sort of pain. He reveled in my cries of agony.

What Nettie suggests is just as terrible. I know it is wrong to even consider it, that I endanger my very soul, but what else am I to do? I have prayed and prayed for guidance, but even God has forsaken me in my hour of need.

There is a price for this, as well. The price is steep, frighteningly so, but my choices are few. Nettie has been with Jonas for over twenty years. In all that time, he has never sired a child. She informs me that Jonas always blames the woman, that it never ends well for them. I am his fifth wife. If I do this, I will be free of Jonas, but bound to something that could be far worse.

What should I do?

1784, August 10

It took me a week to recover. The beating was so severe, I lay abed for days. Nettie says that several of my ribs were broken which is why I had such difficulty breathing. She was concerned I would not live through that first night.

Jonas's anger knows no bounds. I tripped and spilled his tea. For that I was beaten to within an inch of my life. I cannot do this anymore. I will not.

I have asked Nettie to arrange a meeting. I will speak to him.

1784, August 19

His name is Silas. His eyes are a deep black, but I can see the fires of hell in them. Jonas makes me fear for my life, Silas makes me fear for my soul. I know what he is, but I am drawn to him anyway. Mayhap that is the lure of this unnatural attraction. I know I mustn't, but I know I will. Nettie is concerned I have not strength to refuse him anything. I have made no promises, no deals and already he owns me.

Butterflies dance in my stomach when he looks at me and fire races through my veins when he kisses me. His kiss is everything I have ever dreamed of. Nettie tells me I am in lust, but I think I am in love. God help me if that is true, for I know what the outcome is going to be.

He promises me an end to the pain and

humiliation at Jonas's hands, but dare I do it? I will be condemning my own soul if I do this. If I make this deal with him, I will garner everything I have ever wanted and dreamed of and Jonas will never harm me or another woman ever again.

But if I do this, I am damning myself, my children, my grandchildren. For everything I can gain for them, they will be forever cursed, forever damned. Can I do that to them?

1784, September 3
The smell has returned to the house. Jonas has gotten even more secretive, secluding himself in his study for days at a time. There are strange and unsettling noises that come from his study when he is in there, the doors locked. I have even seen bright flickers of light. What is he doing?

I am so unsettled that I jump at every sound. I feel as if I am being watched when no one is there. Sounds keep me up at night. Sometimes I think it is my own guilty conscience that makes me hear these things. I have committed a sin against my husband. I gave in to Silas, and despite all the pleasure gained from that encounter, I cannot shake the guilt of what I have done.

Sometimes I think Jonas knows about my indiscretion. It is the way he looks at me when he thinks I am not aware of it. He gives me a very calculating look, as if he is gambling with my fate himself. Perhaps he has found out and is planning my demise. Mayhap I will find myself thrown into the swamp, left for the animals to feed on my bones.

I sound so very maudlin these days. I am tired, weak, and very disheartened. It is hard for me to get up each morning, but I do it with Nettie's help. There are days I yearn for my death, for an escape from this world, the pain of each day.

I do not understand this malady I am suffering from. It has worsened this week. I found myself staring down from the attic window this morning contemplating how fast my life would end if I just fell. This is not me, but I cannot shake this melancholy. I wish Silas would return to me. He is my only solace. When I am with him, this dreaded feeling goes away. Why is that?

Mayhap Nettie will know what is wrong with me. I shall ask her this eve.

1784, September 22

I have done it, I have damned us all. My prayers have gone unanswered and I had no choice. I overheard Jonas speaking with someone in his study. The other voice, it was vile and it grated on the ears. He was going to kill me for it, to cement his everlasting life.

Before meeting Silas, I would have scoffed at the thought of what Jonas planned. I would never have believed it possible, but now, now I know what he planned for me was very real. I had to save myself if God would not. I made my deal with Silas.

Jonas will require care until the day he dies, but that can be arranged. I have a child growing within me, have had it since that first night with Silas. No one will ever suspect Jonas is not my son's father.

Jonas's body has turned on him. He is trapped inside, unable to speak or move. Death will be a mercy visited upon him. His mind is fully functional, though. He glares at me in hatred every time I walk into the room. I told him about the baby, that he was not the father. I don't know why I did. Perhaps to seek retribution for all that he has put me through these many months. It is of no matter. There is nothing he can do to harm me ever again.

1784, November 11

I am beginning to increase with the child that grows under my heart. Nettie is afraid of the babe growing within me. The original deal was never for it to be Silas's child, but for Jonas to be able to sire a child. I am glad my son will not have Jonas's blood running through his veins. The man is evil. His body grows weaker every day even as my son grows stronger. Soon his life will sputter out and we will be rid of him forever. It is a day I look forward to.

1784, December 3

I accepted condolences from the city as I stood in the cemetery today. Jonas passed from this world two days ago. I must pretend to be sad, but inside I am laughing. I know 'tis wrong, but I cannot help myself. After all the pain and torture I endured at his hands, I am grateful he is gone. No, I am full of joy and happiness he is out of our lives for good.

The plantation is doing well under Mr. Moore's supervision. Our attorney made the arrangements for me and all I have to do is receive the reports once a month on how the property is prospering. I have made several new friends amongst the Americans, of all people. The Creoles snubbed me, thanks to Jonas, so I went out and forged my own friendships. These Americans are remarkable people, not at all the barbarians they were painted in England. The women have welcomed me into their inner circle and I am so grateful to have friends here.

Since that awful day in England, my life has been one unhappy event after another, one struggle after another, and now things are starting to look up. Once Jonas was unable to speak, my melancholy disappeared. I believe he was responsible for it and once he was unable to influence me, the feeling departed.

Thank you, Silas, for giving me

everything I could ever want.

1785, February 9
Several of the servants have fled. I cannot blame them. We are being stalked within the house. It is the only way I can describe it. The odor permeates every orifice in the house and we cannot escape the strange occurrences. Footsteps run up and down the stairs. Candles go out at the oddest of times. The kitchens have been plagued by one horror after another. Three of the staff have died due to accidents. Nettie is even thinking of leaving me. She says our house has been infested. I tell her that is nonsense, but deep down I think she may be right.

Jonas was dealing with demons, but so was I. We invited evil into our home. We opened it up for a possession. What are we to do to combat it?

1785, May 23
It has been so long since I had the strength of will to put thought to paper. My son was born just moments ago. I have named him Jonathan Nathanial Sinclair, although I am sure his new family will change it. I held him for but a few seconds and then sent him and Nettie away from this cursed house. She promised to see him taken care of. I hired an attorney to make all the arrangements and ensured Nettie could stay with my son. She is terrified of

him, but she will keep him safe. She swore it to me. Wherever you go, my beautiful boy, you will be safe.

We discovered the presence stalking us was Jonas. His spirit walks these halls and I know without any hesitation he would have murdered my child. He has made several attempts to cause his death before Jonathan was ever born. There were several close calls.

I am dying. The birthing was hard on me and I am bleeding too much. The doctor says there is nothing he can do. I am using the last of my strength to warn anyone who enters this cursed ground to flee, run fast from here.

Jonas will never leave this place and inflict pain upon its residents for an eternity. He has truly cost me everything.

Do not let him do the same to you.

Chapter Twenty-Two

I close the journal softly and look up. The guys are still whispering in the far corner of the library, unaware of the journal I've discovered. I will bet anything that my soul sucking ghost is Jonas. It makes sense if he made a deal with a demon. I shake my head. Deals with demons? It sounds ridiculous. Can demons do that? Appear human and make a deal to damn your soul in return for something you want more than anything?

In Elizabeth's situation, I can almost agree with her. If I were helpless and in her shoes, I might have done the same thing. Women who lived in the 1700s were considered chattel, the property of their husbands. They had no rights to speak of and in some cases were badly abused by their husbands. Poor Elizabeth. I can almost feel her pain in the words she wrote. Her handwriting told her story. She went from angry, to sad and confused, then to desperate. It's a feeling I'm all too familiar with.

Reading her story makes me think of all the things I have felt since I woke up in this house.

Both Elizabeth and her husband were dealing with demons. Is that why she experienced what she did in the house? I think I remember Doc saying something about demonic infestation in one of his lectures I'd attended. There were three stages I think, but what?

"Doc?" I ask, my voice loud in the hushed whispers going on around me.

Instantly all eyes are on me, worried and concerned.

"Yes, Mattie?" Doc looks the most worried about me except for maybe Dan. Doc understands this gift so much better than I do, so maybe he knows there's a reason to be worried. At this point, I don't care. I just want the ghost responsible for killing Eric to pay a thousand times over.

"Didn't you say there were stages when it came to demons and human activity?"

"Yes." He nods slowly. "Infestation, oppression, and possession. Why?"

"Does the third stage have to be possession, or could it just be a demon lurking about looking to make a deal?"

"How do you know about deals, Mattie?" Mr. Malone asks. "That isn't common knowledge. Only humans who've made deals and my kind know about it."

I handed him the journal and gave him a quick outline of what was in it. "I think they both made deals, but if the demon moved on, then why does the house still mimic the stages of activity?"

"Hold up." Eli frowns at me. "Out of every book in this frickin' library, you pick up the one that talks about deals?"

Dan laughs. "She's really good at this stuff. I keep telling her she'll make a great cop when she graduates."

"In your dreams, Officer Dan." I scowl at him. "You've seen my rap sheet. Police stations and I don't mix very well."

"You've got a rap sheet?" Eli grins. "Well, now, I think you just got a whole lot more interesting, Hilda."

"What did I tell you about calling me Hilda?" I ask through clenched teeth. I can deal with anger so much better than grief.

"Mattie," Doc interrupts Eli before he can stick his foot further in his mouth. "The journal you found belongs to the wife of the original owner of the house. He had it built about a year before he married her. Everything going on with this house started with them."

"Yeah, Doc, I think we figured that out already," Eli says with a hint of sarcasm.

The annoyed look Dan and Caleb give their brother has my eyes widening. It's identical, and in that moment, it's so easy to see they are brothers. I'm not the only one to see it, either. Eli blinks several times and then shakes his head as if to clear it, but the similarities between Dan and Caleb are too strong to ignore.

"I would say that Jonas made a deal for eternal life, but his wife's deal trumped it," Mr. Malone says thoughtfully. "The demon he made the deal with couldn't un-ring the bell, so maybe he gave Jonas eternal life through the ghosts trapped here?

As long as he's able to siphon energy off them, he can maintain his base of power."

"Old Jonas is having issues with that," I tell them. "He's losing his hold on some of the ghosts in residence. He told me that they're growing as strong as him."

"And that's why he wants you," Mr. Malone's shrewd gaze centers on me. "Doc says you are made up of ghost energy, a beacon of shining light to lost souls. If he has you, he can pull more ghosts in and feed off you for an eternity, he'd cement his power."

"That's exactly what he said," I agree, "and that's exactly why we have to stop him."

"Mattie, it wouldn't only be him we'd have to contend with." Mr. Malone sighs. "There seem to be a lot of the bad ones here. You've met some of them."

"Yeah, there are a lot of bad ones." I nod. "But there are so many that are just lost. They call to me and I can't ignore them, not after what I felt, what he did to me." I shudder at the memory of all that despair that consumed me. I was ready to give up after a couple hours. I can't even begin to imagine what these other ghosts have gone through for God knows how long.

"Your gift is still working properly, then?" Doc asks, relieved. "I was worried that the tattoo the boys gave you would cause it to have issues."

"It was hard at first," I tell him. "Took me a minute to figure out how to hear only one voice in the hushed whispers, but piece of cake now."

"So we just need to find his bones and torch

him," Caleb says. "If he was buried in the cemetery, it shouldn't be too hard."

"It's never that easy," I say. "This guy, he's twisted, Caleb."

"Mattie's right," Doc interrupts us. "I did a lot of research into the history of the house and its occupants. Jonas Sinclair was rumored to be of the devil himself, dabbling in sorcery and alchemy."

"But he's dead," Dan interjects. "Doesn't that mean he can't do as much damage as he could before?"

Caleb and Eli both stare at him as if he's a simpleton. Dan has never wanted any part of the supernatural world, but because of me, he's had to learn about it. He just doesn't want to wrap his head around it or he'd know better than to ask that question. Just because you die doesn't mean you've lost your hold on anything.

"And how long have you been hanging out with the ghost chick?" Eli asks, his voice full of derision.

Dan glares at his brother. "It's my fault I didn't grow up a freak show like you?"

I wince. Does he think I'm a freak show, too?

"Brilliant," Eli sighs, looking right at me. "Now you've upset Mattie…again."

Dan whirls to face me. I try to keep my expression as blank as possible, but he knows me too well.

"Mattie, I didn't mean you…"

Whatever," I wave it off. There isn't time to think about it right now. "Back to getting rid of Jonas. Why do you burn the bones?"

"His bones are a physical part of him," Mr.

Malone explains. "They keep him anchored to this plane of existence. If we destroy the bones, his anchor goes away and he moves on."

"So all the ghosts I see are anchored here because of their bones?"

"Not necessarily *just* the bones," Mr. Malone tells me. "It just has to be something with a strong emotional or physical tie to the ghost."

"Something like this house?" I ask. "He's spent a long time here, this house is his power base."

Mr. Malone frowns. "Well, it just got a little complicated."

"You don't say?" I ask sarcastically. "Considering he probably knows exactly what we're planning, what would you suggest?"

"No element of surprise," Caleb muses, "but what if we split up? Two of us take the bones and the rest of us stay here and combat the house?"

"You make it sound like we're going to war," Dan scoffs.

"We are, little brother." Caleb grins. "Welcome to the family business."

Chapter Twenty-Three

Dan pitched a fit when Caleb suggested he go to the cemetery with him, leaving me here at the house. It's not like I can leave. Jonas isn't going to willingly let me out of this house. He plans on feasting off me, which means I have to die. Dan has no idea how to combat a vengeful spirit, especially one that made a deal with a demon. Caleb was right to make him leave. He'll only get in the way of what we need to do here.

What that is, though, I don't know. Eli, his dad, and Doc have been clustered together in the corner since Dan and Caleb left. I asked where Ben was and discovered Mr. Malone sent his youngest son back to the hotel with his mom earlier. That's why I hadn't seen him all night. I'm glad the kid's safe from this mess. I know he's probably used to it, but I don't think it's something someone so young should have to deal with.

I know there's talk about burning the house down, but I don't think it'll work. It's not only the house. There's a cellar, a barn, slave quarters, and numerous other buildings on the property. We can't burn it all down. Personally, I think our best bet is Eli's sword. Jonas ran from it earlier. The problem is getting it close enough to him to do some damage.

"How you holding up?" Eli asks, startling me.

"Peachy," I tell him. "You guys come up with a plan?"

"Dad wants to burn it down, but it's not gonna work." Eli shakes his head. "There's too many buildings he could have left a piece of his DNA in."

"I had the same thought." I nod in agreement.

"We're having a hard time coming up with an alternative plan. Our usual smash and bash isn't gonna work here."

"There's one thing I can try," I say hesitantly. It's not something I want to do and I'm not sure I can since they put that tattoo on me. "I can ask the ghosts in the house. They may or may not answer."

"That's not a bad idea, Mattie," Mr. Malone says from behind us. "A séance could cause a lot of unwanted problems, though. There are bad things in this house that could use it, too."

"You're looking at the ultimate Ouija board standing in front of you," I remind him. "No need for a séance. I just have to open myself up and ask."

"Can you still do that?" Doc asks. "Will the tattoo let her do that?"

Mr. Malone shrugs. "It didn't alter her abilities, only gave her a buffer to them until she learns to control them. If she was talking to a ghost earlier, I'd say she's on her way to doing that, but I'm not sure if it'll hinder her from talking to all the ghosts at once or not."

"Won't know till we try," I tell them.

"Do you need anything in particular?" Mr. Malone asks me.

"Just quiet so I can concentrate." I go over and plop down on one of the couches. "I've only done this once before and those ghosts wanted to talk to me, so I'm not sure it'll work here or not."

Mr. Malone nods and he and Doc take a seat on the other couch. Eli settles himself beside me. I ignore the queasy feeling his presence causes and instead close my eyes.

The room is quiet and I let myself relax. I can feel the energy in me that allows me to speak to the ghosts. I've been getting better at accessing it since my time as a hostage. I grasp hold of it and let it spread through my body, and when I feel it reach my hands, I let it spiral outward, encompassing the whole of the property. The ghosts can feel my power and are drawn to it, like a moth to a flame. They are unable to escape my call.

Cold creeps into me, burning me, as the spirits flood the house. The air turns frigid and I can hear the kitchen sink down the hall start to run. I know without looking that every window and mirror in the room have iced over. I'm shaking from cold and Eli pulls me onto his lap, wrapping me in his heat. For once it actually lessens the pain of the cold, it takes the edge off. Odd, that's never happened before.

"I need help," I call out to them, speaking in my head. *"I want to help you, to free you from this place, but I need your help to do that."*

Immediately, I'm bombarded on all sides and my head explodes in pain. *"Stop, stop,"* I say. *"Not everyone at once, I can't understand you all."*

Instant relief. I'm shocked they stopped so quickly, but then again, I'm offering them freedom.

"How can you help us? We have been trapped here for an eternity."

I open my eyes and see a man of about forty or so standing in front of me. He's wearing an old bowler hat, his pants and shirt so reminiscent of the 1920's. I blink. Moonshine runner is my first thought. He grins at me and nods.

"How did you die?" I ask him.

"My brother and I were coming back from a run and we got shot by the sheriff. We was in a territory we didn't know, so we didn't know how to dodge him. Ed lived and I died."

I love his accent. His i's were stressed, giving his speech the quaint charm of the mountains. *"You were a long way from home if you were in New Orleans."*

"New Orleans?" he asks, confused. *"No, we was up in Virginia when we got caught."*

"Then how did you get here?" I ask, just as confused. *"We're in New Orleans right now."*

He frowns, thinking. *"When I died, I saw this bright light. It felt good, peaceful like, and I remember walking toward it and then...then I was here in this house and Jonas was telling me I had to do penance for what I did in life. I did some bad things, ma'am. I deserve penance, but not this. He hurts us all the time and we've tried to stop him, but we can't. It ain't right, all us suffering like this."*

"I didn't do anything wrong," a woman spoke up. *"I was in a car crash in Arizona and ended up here."*

She is standing across from us, wearing jeans and a Poison tee shirt. Her blonde hair is all frizzed and puffed up like they wore back in the nineties. Her face is bleeding from a cut above her eye and several others covering the entire surface of her face. That's not what killed her, though. It has to be the long shard of glass firmly lodged into her throat. My guess is she went through the windshield.

"What did Jonas tell you?" I ask curiously.

"Only that I was now a part of his family. I tried to leave, but there's a barrier up around the house. It won't let us out."

That I didn't know. I focus my thoughts and try to push outside the property. I can get through easily enough. Why can't they?

I can hear them then, all of them, wailing in the background. They're suffering so much and the reaper in me needs to help them, but how? I can't shake the knowledge I know how to help them and it frustrates me that I can't figure it out.

What I can do is open a doorway to the Between, the place between the living and the dead. A reaper usually ferries the soul through the Between as they pass from this plane to the next. There are very bad things in the Between that would gobble up a poor lost soul. If I open that up, I'd be condemning them to a worse fate than here.

"My friends and I are trying to destroy Jonas," I tell them, *"but we don't know where he hides. If we can find him, we can kill him."*

"You can't kill him," another voice pops up. *"He's too strong. If you try, you'll get killed same as us and then no one can help us."*

That voice belongs to a little boy of about ten or so. His skin is a dark ebony color and he's sitting next to Doc, swinging his legs back and forth. His face is haunted and his eyes are bruised. There's no obvious death wound on him, though, so I'm not sure how he died.

"How did you get here, sweetheart?" I ask him softly.

"I died here." He shrugs. *"We didn't have enough food and I had to give mine up for the little kids. I went to sleep one night and woke up here in the big house."*

My heart goes out to him and I want to make everything all better. He's only a little boy and I can see the suffering in his eyes. Jonas has been keeping them afraid, feeding off their fear for God knows how long. It isn't right, not at all.

"Emma Rose, have you learned nothing?"

My head snaps around to see the painter lounging in the corner. His black eyes are shining with something like frustrated anger. How is he here? I thought he was only in my dreams.

"Dreams are easier to reach you in, but when you open yourself up like this, you let us all in, even Jonas. Don't you feel it? He's starting to drain you again."

I close my eyes again and search for something off. I hadn't felt anything, but then again, I'd been too busy listening to the ghosts. Ah, he's right. I can even see it. My energy is being siphoned, pulled out from me and down the hall.

Wait, if I follow it, I can find him.

"Yes, you can find him, but unless you deplete his power base, you can do nothing to stop him," the painter tells me.

"Why do you care?" I ask him. It's odd that he's trying to help me. Then again, I don't think he's ever really tried to hurt me, either. Sure, he's scared me before, but he's never tried to kill me.

His smile sends shivers up my spine. It promises so much and nothing good. *"I have a vested interest in you, Emma Rose, and I mean to see you safe until I collect you."*

The threat is obvious and sets my own hackles rising. *"Look here, buster..."*

"Shush, child," he says, his own irritation as obvious as my own. *"I'm trying to help you."*

I shut my mouth.

"Good. To deplete his power base, you have to cross the souls over."

"I don't know how to do that."

"Yes, you do," he counters. *"You've done it before without even thinking about it. Think back to that day in the group home, the day all those ghosts were able to leave. You thought it was because the woman died, but as you know now, she was very much alive. It was all you, Emma. You opened that portal for them."*

"Why do you keep calling me Emma?"

"Because it's your name, of course."

"You know who I am?"

Instead of answering, he continues as if I hadn't asked the question. *"You can open the door to the*

Between easily enough, but the portal to cross over is entirely different. That portal opens up and allows other reapers to help the souls to the next plane."

"How do I do it?"

He sighs. *"I'm not a reaper and so I can't tell you. The answer is inside of you. Just think back to that day, think about what you did, what you were feeling. Let it flow from there."*

That day is *not* something I like to think about, but if it will help these people, I'll try.

One of the many therapists I have been to over the years taught me a technique to remember things I don't want to. You take a physical reminder of a memory and use it to recall things you don't want to. I pretty much blocked out everything about that day, but I need those memories now.

I look down at my hands. They are scarred and slightly misshapen. A sledge hammer destroyed them. Mrs. Olson had done it while I'd been strapped down to a chair, unable to help myself. I open and close my fists, feeling the pain it still causes me and I remember running, my ankle twisted and my knee out of socket. The fear eats at me, makes me start to shake with the reminder of how helpless I felt.

I remember Mrs. Olson falling over the railing and I remember sinking down, thinking I was dying. I remember all those ghosts who had helped me despite their fear, but mostly I remember Eric. He'd sat with me, held my hand, and told me it was going to be okay, that he was there with me. I'd felt safe and loved and so peaceful. It had been okay. We would cross over together.

There's a gasp and the voices start to crowd in on me again, all of them excited and afraid.

I open my eyes and I see it. One of the walls has turned into a tunnel of soft, glowing light. I did it. Ohmygosh, I did it.

"It's okay," I tell them. "That's where you're supposed to be. You need to cross over. Go into the light. Someone is waiting for you there."

"*I see my brother!*" the moonshiner says, excitement in his voice. "*He says he's been waiting for me for a long time.*"

"Then go," I tell him with a smile. Once he crosses into the light, the others begin to follow. They are like a stampede set loose. I can feel them flow from this world to the next. Hundreds of them.

"*They're coming, Emma Rose,*" the painter whispers in my ear. "*His guard is on the way. Tell them to be ready to defend you. You have to finish this or you can't defeat Jonas.*"

"Eli!"

"Yeah?"

His voice sounds a bit hushed. I glance at him. He and his dad are both staring at the portal with awe. They can see it?

"You see that?"

He nods. "It's beautiful. You did it?"

"Yeah," I tell him, "but we got problems. Jonas is sending his nasties in to stop me from helping the ghosts cross over. If we don't drain his power, we can't defeat him. You have to keep them away from me until I finish this."

He turns those beautiful aqua eyes to me and

there's something dark and forbidden in them. His face is hard and determined. He's so beautiful in this moment, it hurts my eyes to look at him.

"They won't touch you."

He and his dad stand, swords drawn, as the doors to the library are blown open.

God help us now.

Chapter Twenty-Four

Ax-man from the hallway lumbers toward me, swinging his bloody weapon. The grin on his face makes me flinch on the inside. I can see his ax sinking into me, blood flying everywhere. My heartbeat speeds up and it's all I can do to breathe. I know this ghost can cause me physical harm and that he wants to hurt me. The need to hurt, to maim pours off him in waves. I step back, terrified. The portal on the wall falters, starts to fade.

"No, Emma, don't think about him, just focus on the portal, think of what made it open to begin with," the painter whispers to me.

Easier said than done. He's not the one with a maniac barreling down on him.

Eli steps in front of me and distracts the ghost, giving me a chance to calm down and breathe. I close my eyes, blocking out the ghosts streaming through the door. I need to trust that Eli and his dad will take care of the farmer and the others.

I think about Eric and how safe he always made me feel. My thoughts turn to Dan against my better judgment. He and Eric are the only two people in the world who have ever made me feel safe. They are always there when I need them. Dan is my rock, my one constant. He's why I'm still sane after everything that's happened to me and I understand in this moment that no matter what happens in the future, he'll always be important to me and I can't just throw everything we have away. If that means only being friends, then that's what I'll be. He needs me as much as I need him.

Heat begins to burn through me, melting the ice that's settled in my bones. Fire encompasses my body and for the first time since I was five years old, I'm warm. Really and truly *warm*. I can feel something pulsing, pulling me toward the heat. I'm terrified to open my eyes, but at the same time, I need to know what this is.

The first thing I am aware of is a hum, it's whizzing back and forth, and as I open my eyes, a bright, blinding light assaults me. Blinking, I see Eli and his dad hacking away at the ghosts trying to make their way to me. They are awful to look at, bloody and deformed, but it's Eli who captures my attention. The light around him is so pure a white, it glitters blue, reminding me of the blue tint surrounding a fire's flame. It's beautiful.

The heat I feel is radiating from Eli and into me through a string of light that connects us. I have left my psyche wide open and I can feel things I couldn't before. There's a connection between us that's hard to define, has been there from the moment I met him, and has probably been there since I was born. I have always been restless, the need to constantly roam eating away at me. My mother's penchant to move us from place to place was where I usually put the blame, but now I think it was something else.

I think the chain between us has been pulling us together since forever. I remember back when I ran away from Jersey, I convinced myself that it was because of the foster home I was in. Granted it had been a bad one, but not awful enough to warrant running away. I felt this need to leave, to run toward something. That something is standing in front of me. I know this, like I know Dan is my anchor.

Eli is home. The realization floors me. How can this be? I don't even know him, but he smells of home, makes me think of warm vanilla and sugar cookies, a scent I have always equated with home. I don't know why. My mom wasn't the milk and cookies kind of mom, but that's what I think of when I think of home.

He turns to stare at me, his aqua eyes glowing with a dark light. He looks dangerous and deadly, but instead of making me feel cautious, I feel safe and loved. Odd. He grins that stupid cocky grin of his and I laugh. His shoves his sword behind him without looking, and the ghost attacking him goes poof into soot and ash. It's scary to watch, but I'm calmer right now than I've ever been.

"You have to go, Emma Rose," the painter interrupts my revelations. *"His bones have been salted and burned. You crossed the last innocent soul over and he's weak. You can kill him now."*

"How?" I ask.

"Just follow the trail and you'll know how," he

says. *"Go, now, before it's too late."*

I look back to where Eli and his dad are still fighting and before I can call out to them, I'm being shoved out of the room.

"There's no time to wait on them," the painter tells me as he pushes me along. He feels as real as me. His skin is flesh and bone. What in the world?

The next thing I know I'm in a hallway I've never seen before, but the light leading from me is going around the corner. I can't believe I'm heading into another dangerous situation without weapons or a phone. Didn't I promise Dan to never do that again? I can at least blame it on the ghost this time. Maybe. I'm not sure the painter is a ghost anymore.

The lighting is dim and freaks me out a bit. It reminds me of all those haunted house movies I watched growing up. You'd think it wouldn't bother me considering everything I've seen in the ghost department over the last twelve years, but it does. I feel like I'm *in* one of those cheesy B-rated horror flicks as I walk slowly down the hallway.

The doors creak open as I pass them and the cold seeps out and follows me. It's not really the cold, but more of Jonas's guard. If I turn around, God knows what I'll see and I might even lose my nerve now that all the innocent ghosts are gone. What's to stop Jonas from collecting more souls, though, if I don't stop him? Nothing. All that stands between him and his next victim is me. I laugh, but it's a nervous laugh. His next potential victim is me.

There's a door at the end of the next hallway and the stream of energy goes through the door. The closer I get to it, the harder it is to put one foot in front of the other. I'm tired. That should be a shocking realization, but it isn't a surprise. I've just crossed over hundreds of ghosts while my own energy was being drained. When I finally find Jonas, am I even going to have the energy to fight him? And how can I fight him with no weapon? Is it even possible to defeat him? He's gotten so much stronger than me.

My footsteps falter a little when I open the door and start down the stairs. It must be the basement of the house. I catch hold of the old railing for balance while trying to talk myself out of going down into the darkness. There are no lights here, but I can see because of the glow of my own essence being pulled from me. I should be upset or worried, but I'm not.

There's a problem here, I know it deep down. The way I'm feeling is wrong. I don't care about anything, not even myself. I'm not afraid anymore, just resigned. Jonas is not only draining my soul, he's draining my will to live.

When I step down into the basement, I see him. He's standing amongst a crew of his cronies, smiling at me.

I am exactly where he's wanted me from the moment I stepped foot on the property—in his lair, alone, and helpless.

Chapter Twenty-Five

"Well, well..." He smiles and I shiver. His face is twisted, bloated almost. I don't think he realizes his leftovers are all gone or that his bones have been burned. This should make me feel triumphant, but it doesn't. I can't seem to muster up anything other than nonchalance.

"You are braver than I thought," Jonas tells me. *"I assumed you'd come looking with your own guard."*

"Why?" I ask him. "I don't need them."

"No." He shakes his head. *"You don't need them to die."*

"Am I dying?"

"Yes, you are, my dear." He nods. *"Soon you'll be with me and I will have all the power I need."*

"You're dying too," I tell him. "Don't you feel it?"

"Nonsense." He smiles. *"I'm getting stronger by the second."*

"You haven't noticed all the innocent ghosts are missing or that your bones have been salted and burned?"

He laughs outright. *"My dear girl, you have no idea of your value, do you? I sent my weakest to battle your guards, knowing they would fail, knowing you would cross over the souls that were too weak to do me any more good. The two imbeciles who thought to destroy me by burning my bones meant nothing to me. You are all I need. Your light will power me for an eternity. I can collect new souls, better, stronger souls, now that I have you. I am undefeatable."*

"Emma Rose, you need to snap out of this," the painter hisses in my ear. *"You are a fighter, fight this."*

"Why?" I ask the painter. "This is much easier."

Jonas narrows his eyes at me. *"Who are you speaking to, girl?"*

"He can't hear you?" I ask the painter.

"No," he tells me. *"The only person who can see or hear me is you."*

Hmm…my own little devil on my shoulder. It makes me laugh. I get a devil instead of an angel. It fits, though. I've never been an angel. I've always caused more trouble than I could easily get myself out of. My smart mouth got me into so much trouble.

"There you are," the painter sighs. *"Think about that girl, Emma Rose, think about the girl who has always fought everyone. Wake up, child, wake up and fight."*

"I suppose it does not matter to whom you are speaking," Jonas muses. *"You will be dead soon enough and then I will consume those silly boys*

upstairs. Ah, good, the other two are back. What is the saying, the more the merrier?"

My head snaps back up at that. "You will not touch them."

Jonas laughed. *"So protective of the lads, are you? You have barely any strength left, girl. There is nothing you can do to stop me from consuming them."*

The thought of this…this thing harming Dan or Eli sets my blood to boiling. No one will harm them while there is a breath left in my body. Especially not some ghost with a god complex.

"Oh, there's plenty I can do," I whisper and force my feet to move forward. They are heavy and it hurts to move, but I push on. He will not hurt them.

Jonas sighs. *"You must learn not to fight me. It will only cause you more pain in the long run."*

A blast of air hits me and I can feel myself picked up and thrown backward. My entire body hits the wall of the basement. It is made of some kind of thin wood. The planks splinter with the force of my body and I slide down them, dazed and in a lot of pain. I heard a crack and I'm not sure if it was me or the wall. My head is fuzzy and my vision is a little blurry. My fingers reach up slowly and come away bloody. There is a cut above my eye dripping down into my eyes.

Shaking my head, I stand up. It hurts like the devil, but at least I'm awake now. Losing your soul is the equivalent of losing your will to live, but threaten Dan and all bets are off.

"That the best you can do?" I taunt, my voice low and rougher than I've ever heard it.

"Oh, look, Tavis," Jonas laughs. *"The little girl wants to play. Why don't you show her what happens to little girls who misbehave?"*

The pervy ghost from the hallway saunters toward me. His eyes are full of the promise of pain. He likes to hurt little girls and for a moment, I'm afraid, but only for a moment. I have to protect my boys. Jonas will not touch them.

He strokes my cheek and I force back the shudder it causes. He recks of rot and I gag slightly. Fingers grip my arm and I wince at their strength. I'm so gonna have bruises later. Cold snakes up my arm, but instead of fighting it like I usually do, I embrace it, let it in and welcome it. The cold is the Between and that's where Mr. Pervy is going.

I think about the despair I felt earlier, the panic and helplessness. I think about Eric dying at my feet, becoming a part of me. I'll never see his face or hear him laugh again. Pain wrenches through me and I hold onto to it, nurse it and wrap it around the cold inside me.

There. I see the first faint flickers of that snowy, staticky…something…begin to appear behind him. It grows, becoming larger and larger. Jonas shouts a warning, but he's too late. I use every ounce of strength I have and shove Mr. Pervy into the Between. He falls, arms flying as he tries to stop himself from falling backward, but he can't.

The Between is a place full of scary things that are much, much scarier than Mr. Pervy and he knows it. He stand up warily and tries to step back into this reality, but once in the Between, there is no coming back for a ghost, especially one who has escaped Judgment for so long. I hear the distant wail of a creature. It is the scream of the hunt. Mr. Pervy stares at me for a long minute and then he takes off running.

I turn my attention to Jonas and for the first time since I've met him, he looks a little worried, cautious. As well he should. He's about to become food to one of the beasties that live in the Between.

"No, Emma Rose." The painter stops me with a hand on my shoulder. *"If you send him there, you doom yourself. Your soul is inside of him now, almost all of it. If he goes there, so do you."*

"Then how do I stop him?" I ask silently, aware of the fact Jonas can't hear us.

"You must reap him and send him to be judged."

"I don't want that black soul inside me," I whisper to myself. Eric, I can deal with, but Jonas? No way.

"It is the only way I know to take back your soul."

Why did I know he was gonna say that?

No help for it. I square my shoulders and start toward Jonas, leaving the portal to the Between open. No point in letting him know I can't put him there without risking myself.

"Interesting," Jonas says. He takes a step back and I feel him pulling harder at my soul, making me weaker and weaker.

"Do you know what's in there, Jonas?" I ask him softly. "There is only fear and pain and death in the Between. There are monsters in there that make you look like Mother Theresa. How'd you like a one-way ticket?"

I go flying backward again, my head hitting something sharp. Sharp, jagged pain explodes behind my eyes, but I force myself to stand back up. Jonas is but a blob in a bright haze now. This can't be at all good, but I won't let him near Dan or Eli. Not a snowball's chance in Hades will he ever lay hands on them, not as long as I have breath in my body.

"You just do not learn, do you?" Jonas asks, but I can hear the desperation in his voice. I shouldn't be able to stand, to come at him, yet I am and he's confused.

"You. Will. Not. Touch. Them."

Each word is punctuated with a step forward. The distance between us is eaten up by my slow, methodical steps. I need to touch him. Cold creeps up my back and I know without looking more of his guards are coming at me. I don't stop walking, just focus on the feel of the cold at my back. The tattoo the boys gave me is not only for controlling the voices, I realize. It's helping me focus on more than one ghost at a time. I know exactly how many are behind me and it's easy enough to imagine them being tossed into the Between. I can hear their screams as they fall into the snowy field. Jonas looks truly alarmed by now and it's my turn to smile.

"Never, ever threaten this girl's family," I hiss at him, deflecting more ghosts as they rush at me. Now that I've figured out how to control this part of my gift, it is easy enough to toss them into the Between. They need to be judged and so they shall. "I am a reaper, Jonas, and it is my right to send souls to their judgment. It is long past your reaping and I mean to set that right."

Jonas hisses at me, now understanding exactly what I mean to do. He throws me again, but the closer I get to him, the stronger I become. It is my soul he has inside of him and I want it back. Why can I not consume my own soul the way he is? From a distance? I focus on the energy bleeding out from me into him. I imagine my fingers wrapping around it, pulling it toward me and into me. The flow reverses and I smile wider.

"You're not the only one who can consume energy," I laugh. "You really should have run the moment you saw me because I'm going to be your downfall."

Jonas pulls with all his might, but it's a useless effort. The energy is mine, belongs to me, and therefore responds to me more than it does him. He wails in frustration and I laugh harder. The power rushing into me makes my head spin, makes me feel like nothing can hurt me. It's a heady feeling and I know why he does this. It's addictive. A girl could get used to this.

With a resounding snap, every ounce of my energy flows back into me. Jonas sags, his strength gone.

"Feeling the loss of those souls now?" I ask him snidely. "Your bones are gone and your power base has been obliterated. Time to give it up, old boy."

"Never," he snarls and rushes me. The Between is still open behind me and if I but step aside, he'll run right into that, but I won't let that happen. The Between is too good for him. He has caused more

pain and suffering than most in his life and in his afterlife.

No, it's time for Jonas to face up to his past.

I close the Between and then open another portal before stepping aside. Jonas runs into the light, his arms outstretched to grab me. He stumbles and falls, his face cringing when he sees where he has landed.

A noise begins to vibrate in the basement, a screeching so loud I cover my ears, and I still hear it. There is a figure that walks out of the light and stands over Jonas.

"Elizabeth," he whispers.

"Hello, husband," she snarls. The beautiful golden light darkens and streaks of fire caress Jonas's flesh. He screams and tries to run, but Elizabeth grabs him, holding him close. *"Oh, no, husband. You condemned us the moment you made that deal. Now, it's time to pay the piper."*

There is a slight fissure that opens in the ground beneath them, growing and rumbling. Jonas looks panicked, fighting to get away from Elizabeth, but she's got a grip like a terrier has on a bone he's just stolen. There's no escaping this.

The distinct smell of rotten eggs surrounds us. Sulphur. Sulphur means demons. The crack widens and dark shapes rise up, latching onto Jonas and Elizabeth, dragging them down. Jonas fights the entire way, but Elizabeth only smiles.

"Mattie, look out!"

I hear Eli shout the warning a mere second before hands grip my throat and I can't breathe, can't see, can't do anything.

Sulphur, sulphur, sulphur! Why didn't I realize

it?

My demon stalker.

Chapter Twenty-Six

It's behind me, so I can't see it, but I can smell it. Hands are around my throat squeezing, cutting off my air. A dark sticky substance drips down my shirt. Black goo. So gross. The goo creeps up my neck and into my mouth, choking me. I did not survive Jonas to die at the hands of this freaking cesspool! I struggle to move, to fight, but I'm frozen. Whatever abilities this thing has, it's stronger than I am.

Eli is the first to reach me. Before his glowing blade can slash the demon, it disappears and I fall, spitting out mouthfuls of nasty black slime. Eli catches me before my knees hit the ground. Pausing only long enough to make sure I'm breathing, he whirls back around, looking for the creature.

Dan, Caleb, and Mr. Malone spread out, looking as well. The stench of sulphur is still strong, so I know it's here. We all do, but where?

I see it before anyone else. The thing is right behind Dan and looking at me. It jerks twice, its face almost a mask of glee. Black goo oozes out of its feet and twines around Dan's ankles, causing him to fall. Hands wrap around his shoulders, the black slime snaking out and covering him. I'm up before even I realize it and sprinting toward him.

His eyes tell me to stay back, to stay safe, but not a chance.

Rage settles into a deathly calm and on the edge of my vision, I see that same white light I saw on the porch earlier when the demon attacked us. Whatever abilities I have, I use my ghost senses to reach out, drawing on the energy of the ghosts native to the area. The ones trapped here in the house are gone, but not the ghosts around us. We are in the City of The Dead, after all. The cold rushes in, settles into me and I smile at the demon. It wails in frustrated anger.

The white light begins to coalesce into a shiny bright ball, like a baseball. I imagine it settling into my hands. The cold surrounding that light burns hotter than anything I've ever felt. It singes my hands, but I hold on, refusing to let the pain deter me from saving Dan.

Black goo wraps itself around him, squeezing, and I can see the panic in his eyes. He's terrified and it fuels my own panic. He can't die. I won't let him die. Dan cannot leave me. I don't know what I'd do without him. He's my best friend and I can't lose him, not after having lost everything else in my life. I won't lose him.

My only thought is to save Dan. The energy ball pulses hotter in my hand and I scream from the pain. I can hear the Malones shouting in the background, but I pay them no mind. My only focus is Dan and the demon. I pull my hand back and throw the light at the thing, willing it to strike the demon in the head. Much to my shock, it flies true and lands with a sickening thud against the wet ooze dripping out of every orifice of the creature. The ball engulfs the demon, trapping it, before it explodes into blinding white light all around the demon. Dan is thrown back from the flames now surrounding the thing behind him.

It screams and writhes, but can't escape the fire engulfing it. It only takes a few seconds for it to die in the flames, but it feels like hours to me.

Dan stands up and stares from the ashes to me and then back. His face is full of awe and a little fear. Then again, he's always been slightly terrified of me, I think. It's a wonder he's stuck around this long.

My vision blurs again and I shake my head, suddenly so tired. I don't know what I just did, but whatever it was, it zapped all the energy I had. I sway on my feet and feel Eli catch me again.

Those gorgeous aqua eyes stare into my hazel ones. They are full of fear, not of me, but for me. He should know by now it takes more than a few ghosts and a demon to kill me.

"You found me," I whisper, my voice much hoarser than before. I hadn't expected them to find me so soon.

"Haven't you figured out by now, Hilda, I'll *always* find you?"

"Don't…call me…Hilda." I glare or try to glare at him. The room is getting so much darker. The last thing I hear is the sound of his laugh before I finally give in to the soft, soothing blanket of unconsciousness.

Chapter Twenty-Seven

I wake up to the oh so familiar sound of medical equipment bleeping at me. I know without opening my eyes I landed in the hospital yet again. My entire body aches, but then, I did get thrown against the wall several times by Jonas. My head is killing me, too. I'm fairly certain that if I open my eyes, my poor head will hurt worse. Most people forget to turn down the lights when there's a head injury involved. Instead of opening my eyes, I crack open one, just a bit. Much to my surprise, the room is muted. There is a light on, but it's coming from the bathroom. I open my eyes slowly, letting them adjust to the soft light in the room. It still hurts, but not nearly as much as I expected.

"You're awake."

I turn my head carefully and see Eli sitting on the right side of my bed. A quick check confirms Dan is asleep in a chair on the other side.

"Hey," I murmur. My voice is a little scratchy, but it's to be expected after almost getting choked to death...again.

"How are you feeling?" he asks.

"Like I just got ran over by a demon?"

Eli chuckles. "We were all worried about you."

"Takes more than a ghost and a demon to take me out."

"Yeah, I think you may be right. Do you remember everything that happened?"

I nod. Hard to forget a homicidal ghost who wanted to eat you. "You guys showed up faster than I expected. You find me on Doc's cameras?"

Eli shakes his head and he frowns. "I looked up and you were gone. I ran after you. Not sure how I knew where you were, I just did."

"You're pretty good at finding me," I say. Maybe he saw what I did? Not a snowball's chance am I telling him about that glowing energy rope that bound us together. Probably never will. I'm not sure I'm ready to face what that chain means. I just met him and he aggravates me more than anyone I've ever met, but at the same time, I have this soft spot for him. I need time to think about this.

"Yeah, it's weird." He laughs, his aqua eyes showing his confusion. "I just know where you are, especially when you're in trouble."

"Weird," I agree.

He stares at me and I start to fidget. His lips quirk in a half smile and his eyes turn darker, more intense. I can feel the blush creep up my neck and bloom onto my cheeks. I'm not a blusher, but this boy can make me redder than a cherry. I'm so flustered, I want to snarl at him.

"Hey, Eli...Mattie you're awake!"

We both turn our head to see Caleb come into

the room. He looks so relieved.

"Hi." I smile at him. Caleb reminds me so much of a big brother. It makes me wonder if I have a brother.

"You okay, kid?" he asks and I nod. "Good, we have to get going and I didn't want to drag Eli out of here while you were still out, but we gotta go."

"You guys off to chase another ghost?" I ask them.

"Nope." Eli grins at me. "We're going to Charlotte."

"What?"

"Dad figures we need to get to know our new brother and we should have a home base so Benny can go to school on a regular basis."

Charlotte? He's coming to Charlotte? I thought I'd have time to think, to figure things out, to come to grips with some stuff...but if he's coming to Charlotte...

"Don't look so happy about it." Eli laughs at my panicked look. "We can explore this sick stomach of yours some more..." He laughs out loud at my mortified expression.

"Eli," Caleb warns, but there's a grin lurking. "She's recovering from a concussion. Leave the kid alone."

"Okay." He chuckles and then leans in to give me a chaste kiss on the cheek. "See you in Charlotte, Hilda."

"Don't call me Hilda!" I try to shout after him, but it comes out more a strangled whisper. He and Caleb are laughing as they head out the door. I'm so gonna beat that boy black and blue.

"You really like him, don't you?"

My head whips around to see Dan staring at me, his puppy dog eyes wounded. I wince at the pain that tears through my head. Shouldn't have moved so fast.

"You really like Meg, don't you?" I counter. We both wince at the truth of it.

"Look, Squirt, I really didn't mean to hurt you the way I did. I was trying to protect you and it all got mixed up and I…"

"I forgive you, Officer Dan," I tell him. "Just don't ever lie to me again."

"I swear to you, Mattie, I won't. No matter what, I'll never lie to you again."

"Even by omission of the truth," I warn him.

"I swear."

"What time is your flight?" I ask him. "Did you have to change it for later today? I know you were supposed to fly out this morning but…"

"Mattie, you've been out for two days."

"But your mom—"

"Can wait," he halts me mid-sentence. "I told you I'd never leave you, Squirt, and I won't, no matter how hard you try to push me away. Mom's fine. She's got my brother and Dad. You didn't have anyone but me."

I have Eli. The thought flits through my head and I feel like I'm betraying Officer Dan in some way, but I know that's not true. I do have Eli. I'm just not sure what to do with him or even if I want him yet.

"Well, I'm awake now," I tell him. "You need to be with your family right now."

"You are my family, Mattie." He smiles, his face

tired and worn. "No matter what, me and you, kid, we're always family."

"Agreed, Angel Boy." I laugh at his grimace then ask a serious question. "Do you regret meeting me, Dan? Until you walked into my hospital room, you had no idea about ghosts. Now you have them to deal with, demons, and your mom is in trouble because of me..."

"Stop right there," he tells me and sits up. "What my mother did was awful and that's why she's in jail right now. Not because of you. You did nothing wrong, Squirt. Don't think for a minute you did. And no, I don't regret meeting you. You're my best friend, Mattie, and I honestly don't know what I'd do if you really did cut me out. I went a little nuts when you ran from me. I knew Meg and I would make you mad, but I didn't think for a second it would hurt you like it did. When I saw your face that day..." He runs a nervous hand through his hair. "I could never regret you, Mattie."

Why does he have to do this? Say things like this? It's so confusing. One thing he and I agree on though, is that we are best friends. I can do that.

"Just don't expect me to be nice to Meg," I tell him. "If I see her, I might hit her."

"She won't like it. She thinks you'll get over it because you're friends."

"Yeah, no," I say. "Not gonna happen, Officer Dan."

He nods, accepting that and then laughs when I yawn. "As soon as the doctor says you can go home, I'll book us a flight to Charlotte."

"What do you think about the Malones moving

to Charlotte?" I ask hesitantly.

He shrugs. "I guess we'll just take it one day at time. Get some sleep, Squirt. I'm gonna go call Dad and let him know you're awake. He's been blowing up my phone all day worried about you."

"Tell Mr. R. I said hi," I tell him as he stands up and walks out into the hallway, leaving me alone.

I really am tired. Why is it when you're in the hospital, you sleep? Your body seems to want to rest. I think it's partly psychological, partly because you need to. I'm always up for a good nap, especially after having been knocked around by a ghost.

"Alone at last."

What the...I look to see the painter standing in the doorway to the bathroom. I frown. The room isn't cold, it should be cold. He's a ghost and ghosts generate cold.

"I'm not a ghost." He laughs and takes the seat Dan vacated.

"Then what are you?" I demand.

He only smiles at me. "I'm here to give you a gift, Emma Rose, free and clear."

"A gift?" I ask, confused. "Why?"

"Because you have pleased me so much, my beautiful girl. You'll never understand the things that had to be set into place to ensure your birth and I couldn't be more excited over the results."

"I don't understand...what are you talking about?"

He ignores me as usual and leans forward to grasp my hands. "This should have never happened. Your art is a gift, Emma Rose, and to be denied that gift is by far the worst tragedy to have befallen you."

My hands begin to grow warm and a white hot pain sears them. I yank them out of his and curl them protectively against my chest. "Are you trying to make sure I never draw again?"

"No, Emma. I'm only finishing what you started. When you saved your young friend, you used a part of your soul to do it. While you held it in your hands, it tried to heal them, but you were so focused on killing the demon, you ignored it. I only finished it."

I pull my hands away from my chest and slowly unwrap the left one. My mouth drops open. All the scars are gone and they look as normal as they once did. I wiggle my fingers and there is no pain. Even the pins don't hurt...wait. I run my fingers over my hand and the pins are gone...just gone.

"How?" I whisper.

"You'll learn how to do that yourself soon," he smiles. "Now I must be going. You have to sleep and I have other business to attend to. I am out of paint and need to stock up."

I swallow. I know what his paint is. It's blood. He's going hunting another victim.

"Good-bye, Emma. I'll see you soon."

"Wait!" I shout, causing him to pause. "You never told me your name."

"It's Silas."

He drops that bomb-shell and then he up and freaking poofs out of existence.

I start to hyperventilate.

Silas.

Ohmygod. A demon helped me. Why?

He knows who I am and he said he'd see me soon.

My monitors start to go a little crazy as my blood pressure spikes and my breathing becomes a little labored.

The nurse rushes in and I can't calm down. She shoots something into my IV. My vision starts to blur and darkness creeps into the edges of my vision and I only have one thought before I fall into that dark oblivion of sleep.

Silas.

Acknowledgements

Well, let's see...so many people need a thank you.

First and foremost, my fans deserve a huge shout out. You guys give me so much encouragement every single day and I love you all more than you know.

Mags, you're a doll. Without your help, my work would be riddled with so many errors. You never fail to jump in and help. What would I do without you?

Susan, Ang, and Sheree...you are always there when I need you.

To all the wonderful people at Limitless Publishing, you rock. You always look out for me and are there to help no matter what I need. The authors there have a support network unlike anything I've ever seen and I'm so grateful to have gotten to know many of you.

To my agent, Ricia Mainhardt, for believing in me when so many others didn't.

My family—I don't know how you put up with me when I'm in the zone. But please remember to shove a sandwich at me once in a while.

Thank you all for everything you have done and put up with from me.

About the Author

So who am I? Well, I'm the crazy girl with an imagination that never shuts up. I *love* scary movies. My friends laugh at me when I scare myself watching them and tell me to stop watching them, but who doesn't love to get scared? I grew up in a small town nestled in the southern mountains of West Virginia where I spent days roaming around in the woods, climbing trees, and causing general mayhem. Nights I would stay up reading Nancy Drew by flashlight under the covers until my parents yelled at me to go to sleep.

Growing up in a small town, I learned a lot of values and morals. I also learned parents have spies everywhere and there's always someone to tell your mama you were seen kissing a particular boy on a particular day just a little too long. So when you get grounded, what is there left to do? Read! My Aunt Jo gave me my first real romance novel. It was a romance titled "Lord Margrave's Deception." I remember it fondly. But I also learned I had a deep and abiding love of mysteries and anything paranormal. As I grew up, I started to write just that and would entertain my friends with stories featuring them as main characters.

Now, I live in Huntersville, NC where I entertain my niece and nephew and watch the cats get teased by the birds and laugh myself silly when they swoop down and then dive back up just out of reach. The cats start yelling something fierce…lol.

I love books, I love writing books, and I love entertaining people with my silly stories.

Facebook:
https://www.facebook.com/authorAprylBaker

Twitter:
https://twitter.com/AprylBaker

Wattpad:
http://www.wattpad.com/user/AprylBaker7

Website:
http://www.aprylbaker.com/

Blog:
http://mycrazzycorner.blogspot.com/

TSU:
http://www.tsu.co/Apryl_Baker

Goodreads:
http://www.goodreads.com/author/show/5173683.A
pryl_Baker

Linkedin:
http://www.linkedin.com/pub/april-
baker/44/6b9/3a4

Made in the USA
Las Vegas, NV
14 December 2020